# The girl I met that night

# The girl I met that night

ZAHIR CHAUHAN

Srishti
PUBLISHERS & DISTRIBUTORS

**Srishti Publishers & Distributors**
A unit of AJR Publishing LLP
212A, Peacock Lane
Shahpur Jat, New Delhi – 110 049
editorial@srishtipublishers.com

First published by
Srishti Publishers & Distributors in 2021



10 9 8 7 6 5 4 3 2 1



Printed and bound in India

*Dedicated to all those who
never give up on their dreams.*

Acknowledgments

I thank and express my gratitude to all those who trusted me and kept me motivated in my journey of becoming a storyteller.

A big thank you to all the readers, reviewers and bloggers who showered their love, appreciated my stories, and encouraged me to write more.

My publisher, for showing faith in this book.

Last but not least, my family for their extended support and understanding while I was busy completing this book.

Gratitude... Gratitude... Gratitude.

# *Prologue*

**Ladakh**

It is midnight and the temperature outside has dropped to almost minus. The fog is making the visibility barely possible on the road. One wrong turn and the car can crash into the deep valley.

If I die in the crash, no one would ever come to know what happened to me. But would it matter to anyone? And why should it? Who am I? I barely have anyone in my life. Life has never before been so cruel. I feel choked with each passing day. There is no will to live left in me.

This journey, at this moment, seems like one of the most difficult journeys of my life. But I am not bothered. All I want right now is to make it to the monastery at any cost, even if it takes the life out of me. I need to be there. Anyhow!

We were heading towards the biggest Buddhist monastery of Ladakh. It was my last hope to get back to a normal life.

It seems like a long time ago that I was enjoying a life I had always dreamt of. I had a flourishing career, lots of money and social respect. Everything was so amazing, until fifteen months ago. Fifteen months and twelve days, to be precise! How can I forget what I have been going through since that night!

That night on the highway changed my life completely. Since then, life has been a roller coaster. Why did life offer those magical moments in the beginning when it had to snatch away everything as soon as I began enjoying them?

Look at my condition now! People think I have been gripped by some severe illness, or probably depression. It's not their fault. Anyone would feel that way on seeing my unshaven face, the dark circles due to lack of sleep, my short temperament, and the listless look almost every day. I had started looking older than my actual age.

From a guy who was always a top performer, who got the best business into the company's kitty, whom clients always chose to work with, I was now hardly able to concentrate on anything. In recent times, I had not been able to concentrate on work at all and had not closed any deal for my company.

Oh god! What is happening with my life? Where is my destiny taking me?

"Sir, the jeep won't go beyond this," the driver said, stopping the jeep. "You will have to walk till there," he said, pointing at the few hundred steps that led to the monastery.

"Okay," I said, opening the car door.

"Sir, I will come with you," he offered.

"No, my friend! You have done a lot for me already. From here, I will manage it myself," I replied.

"Okay, but keep this with you. You will need this," he said, handing me a torch.

With the torch in my hand and hope in my heart, I started walking towards the monastery. I was positive that I will find my answers here, but every passing second also increased my restlessness.

The temperature had dropped down to minus now. Despite being a *pahadi* guy, who had spent his entire childhood in Manali, I was not able to tolerate the piercingly cold breeze of the Ladakh valley.

The wind was making the situation worse. I started losing my energy, and because of the lack of oxygen, I felt breathless and started coughing. My hands froze and I couldn't hold myself up any longer. I fell down on my knees on the steps of the monastery.

"You have to reach there, Kabir. You can't leave your journey in between. Just a few more steps and you will be there. Don't give up, Kabir! Get up... get up!" I shouted to myself.

I gathered all my strength and started walking once again, finally reaching the door of the monastery.

"Oh god, no!" The huge wooden door of the monastery was closed.

I had started shivering, having lost all my energy. I began to lose control of my breathing again and I could feel my body getting almost paralyzed. I felt some blood trickle down my nose. Gradually, I was losing myself.

"Anamika... Anamika..." I started shouting, banging on the door. Then, I collapsed.

"Open your eyes, son." I heard a gentle voice

"Ah, my head!" It really hurt.

"Don't worry, you are fine now."

I opened my eyes slowly. I wasn't feeling cold anymore. I saw a fireplace in the room. I was on a wooden bed, tucked in a warm blanket. I saw a monk sitting next to me. He wore a simple red robe, had a big bright forehead, small but sparkling eyes, a peaceful face and a smile which had the feeling of utmost contentment.

"How are you feeling now?" he asked, coming close to me.

"I am ok," I replied, trying to get up.

"Relax! You should rest," he said

"How did I get here?" I asked.

"I heard your voice at the door; you were calling out someone's name. I have spent my life here and haven't seen someone coming in so late. By the time I reached the door, you had already collapsed. I got you here," the monk said.

"Oh, thank you," I said, recollecting the turn of events.

"Don't thank me. God never wanted to let you die, hence you are alive. Be thankful to the almighty," he told me.

I didn't respond to that. I had lost faith in god.

"What happened, son? You look disturbed," he asked, looking at me lovingly. "Are you looking for someone?"

"Yes, I am looking for someone. I have come here in search of her."

"Who?" he asked

"Anamika," I replied

"Anamika?"

"Yes, Anamika. Have you met someone by this name here?" I asked, now restless.

"So many visitors come here every day; we don't really remember their names, son," he said.

"But she wasn't a visitor. She must have come here in search of peace and stayed at the monastery," I clarified.

"Like I said, many people come here. Some stay for a few hours, while others stay longer, for a few days. Since they come here in search of peace, we don't disturb them. Still, if you can tell me more about her, I can probably help you. But, who are you?" he asked with concern.

"I am the unluckiest person in this world, who has probably lost his love forever now," I said with moist eyes.

"Love is not something you can ever lose; it always remains in your heart," he replied with a soothing smile.

Then, after a brief pause, he asked me, "Tell me what has happened. I may not be able to help by solving your problem, but you can pour your heart out. That will surely help you."

His words made sense. I took a deep breath, wrapped the blanket around tighter and began narrating my story.

# 1

## 15 months ago

### Darjeeling

*Ae maalik tere bande hum... Aise ho hamare karam... neki par chale...*

"Oh god, what was that awful noise? It's so early in the morning." My brain protested.

I reached out from under my blanket to switch off the alarm. But the alarm got louder and louder. I desperately tried to catch another ten minutes of sleep to enjoy some moments of comfort. After all, I had pulled an all-nighter to finish the final piece of my proposal. I had to pitch it today to a well-known exporter of interior decorations. Since he had come all the way from Bhutan for the meeting, it was sort of a big deal.

That was not the first time I had stayed up late to complete a client proposal. Ever since I had joined Blenks International Media (BIM) six years ago, working late nights had become a norm. BIM was known for its fantastic and highly appreciated advertisement campaigns, which made its competitors cry and its clients rich. It had a reputed brand name, amazing client list and a stylish office in the commercial hub of Mumbai. The loads of perks and a lucrative salary was the icing on the cake. The team was full of young and dynamic people who left no stone unturned to prove their worth. The motivation levels were high and it couldn't get any better for someone like me, who had started his career with BIM.

Six years ago, as a student in the final semester of my master's in advertising, I was selected by BIM through campus placement. I joined as an Associate Innovator. With my 'can-do' attitude, immense hard work and promising creative ideas, I soon became a blue-eyed boy for the management. I had some kickass ideas which impressed clients so much that they particularly started asking that I must be given their projects. For a middle-class guy who had never seen so much in life, there was no stopping me then. With each passing year, I began to pull ahead from the pack. Eventually, I was able to successfully create an impact and make a name for myself. In fact, I was one of the youngest creative heads of BIM.

Through all those years, my career had been flourishing at a great pace. I had everything I could ask for – a lucrative job, classy lifestyle, lots of money and a rewarding career which drove me to work even harder to achieve newer heights of success. With so much going for me in Mumbai, I knew without a doubt that I was never going back to my hometown, the place where I spent my childhood days – Manali. Mumbai became the land of my dreams where I was going to build my future.

"Oh shit!" I said upon seeing the time on my mobile. It was already 8:00 a.m.

I sprang out of bed and made a beeline to the bathroom. The client meeting was scheduled for 9 a.m. at The Emerald Conference Room of Grand Heritage Hotel, Darjeeling. There was no way I could reach late for my presentation.

Thank god, I had at least one thing going for me that day. I was staying at the same hotel, which meant no traffic woes. All I had to do was get ready and use the elevator to get to the right floor.

By 8:35 a.m., I was ready to go. I quickly shrugged into my black Italian fit suit, grabbed the designer watch and applied the gel on my hair before looking into the mirror.

"Let's do it!" I told myself. I left my room and took the elevator to take me to the hotel lobby.

"May I help you, sir?" The concierge asked as she saw me scanning the signboards in the lobby, searching for the elusive Emerald Room.

"Oh, yes! Can you please help me with the directions to the Emerald Room?" I asked

"It's right there, sir." She smiled as she pointed to a door that had somehow escaped my attention.

"Thanks!"

I rushed towards the door with all haste.

"Good morning, everyone. I'm Kabir." I greeted the men sitting around the table.

"Good morning. I am Sen and this is my team." A gentleman wearing a black coat and a hat came forward and introduced himself.

"My apologies for keeping you waiting, sir."

"No, no, don't be. We walked in only a minute ago, so you are not late, son," he replied politely. "Shall I order some tea or would you prefer some coffee, Kabir?"

"Actually, I wouldn't mind a green lemon tea," I replied while connecting my MacBook with the projector.

Soon, the server arrived and served tea and coffee to everyone present in the room.

After a few minutes of making casual talk, I started my presentation by explaining to them my vision for their advertisement campaign. It was specifically designed to launch their product line of interior decorating products for Indian consumers. This product was supposed to be launched in India with the help of a Malaysian investor and was supposed to be one of the biggest business launches in this stream.

I spent the rest of the day presenting and clarifying the entire advertisement campaign to our client. They requested several changes which led to further discussions and debates. The day was long and hectic, but proved to be very fruitful. I knew this deal would not only result in an inflow of revenue for the company, but also give my career an additional boost.

"So, are we good to go, sir?" I asked, shutting my MacBook.

"Oh, yes! I am very happy with the overall campaign and your proposal, Kabir. I must say I am very impressed. Whatever we had heard about your agency, and especially about you, proved to be 100% correct. You really bring a lot of fresh and innovative ideas to the table," Mr Sen replied.

I thanked him with a smile and looked at my watch. It was already 6:30 p.m.

"Do draft the contract and have the same sent across to my office," Mr Sen summed up.

"Absolutely, sir. I will ask my legal team to have the contract prepared once I reach office tomorrow morning".

"Tomorrow morning? We thought you would stay back and give us a chance to host you tonight."

"Actually, I have to reach Bagdogra to catch the last flight back to Mumbai, sir. I have a few important meetings lined up for tomorrow," I replied looking at the clock.

"Oh, I see! Busy man," he said and smiled.

"Not as big as you, sir."

"I am sure you will be even bigger than me one day," he predicted.

"Thank you, sir. I appreciate your kind words," I replied. I shook hands and took his permission to leave.

I literally ran to my room and quickly loaded my bag with my clothes that were strewn all over the room. After packing my bag, I checked out of the hotel. My cab was waiting in the hotel porch.

I hopped into the car at around 7:30 p.m. prepared for the three-hour ride to Bagdogra. My flight back was scheduled to depart at 11:55 p.m. I was on a very tight schedule.

Soon, the cab started moving on the narrow roads of Darjeeling. The sun had already set and there weren't many people on the road. The shopkeepers were winding up for the day.

Seeing them hustle, I thought to myself. 'What an amazing life these people must have, everything is so simple.' It reminded me of my life back in Manali – peaceful and calm!

Life in Mumbai was a constant struggle. Every day, we got up with the purpose of getting to the office on time and trying to return on time, which eventually never happened.

From losing ourselves in work from the moment we set foot in the office to late evening or even night, we worked dazed and exhausted. And even then, our continued focus was to prepare for the next day. Added to it were the commuting woes for a Mumbaikar!

On the other hand, life was much easier back in Manali. If there were exciting career opportunities, I could have lived there all my life. Now that I had money, the irony was that I didn't have time to enjoy my life.

As I mulled over my life choices, the car left the main town and reached the highway, which was actually carved out of the mountain range. Like any other hill station, the road was twisted around the mountain. The air held the promise of a heavy shower and it soon started to drizzle.

I was exhausted after the day-long meeting and the fact that I hadn't slept very well the previous night didn't help. As a result, I dozed off soon. After about an hour, I was rudely awakened by my cab driver. He was talking pretty loudly in his local language to the driver in the car adjacent to us.

I could not understand a word. It was completely dark outside. As I looked through the window, I could see a long queue of vehicles ahead and beside us. None of the vehicles were moving.

"What happened?" I asked the driver.

"Sir, due to heavy rain, there seems to be a major landslide which has blocked the entire highway."

"Oh! Now what?"

"These people have been waiting here for quite some time now and it seems the traffic is not going to clear up for another few hours," he replied, pointing at the long queue of vehicles.

"What! The entire night?" I yelled in exasperation.

"Yes sir, the landslide is really bad this time. The traffic has really piled up on both sides and it would be impossible to move ahead."

"But I have a flight to catch in a few hours," I said in despair, looking at my watch.

"I know sir, but there isn't anything I can do. You can see the jam ahead," he said pointing towards the downward sloping road. I could see a long trail of vehicles for miles ahead. He was right. I was stuck.

"Can we go back to Darjeeling?" I asked after thinking for a while.

"No sir, the vehicles have created a jam behind us, as also on the adjacent side. It would be difficult to take a U-turn on the narrow road."

"Oh, I see," I said as I looked behind us. "So, what should we do now?"

"We have to wait till they clear the way."

"You mean we are stuck in the cab for a couple of hours or more?"

"Sir, there is a restaurant around a kilometre away. If you don't want to spend hours in this cab, you can walk till there, have food and take some rest. Once the jam gets cleared, I will come and pick you up from the restaurant."

The jam was rather long and was not going to clear anytime soon. It was no point waiting in the cab for hours. At least I could relax and figure something out at the restaurant.

I took my laptop bag and thanked the driver as he handed me his umbrella.

# 2

As per his directions, I started walking towards the restaurant. As I passed the vehicles on either side, I could see frustration and anger in everyone's eyes.

After a few minutes of walking on the road filled with vehicles, I finally reached the restaurant. It was small and cosy. Peering through the glass door, I could see that there were a few old wooden tables and chairs scattered around the room. However, the entire room was filled with people. All of them were stuck here in the middle of nowhere, thanks to the landslide.

Since the inside sitting area was full, I looked at the other side of the restaurant where a few more tables were placed. It was an open sitting area with an almost *kutcha* (mud) roof on top. Most people didn't want to sit there as it was cold and now, the rain was making everything worse.

The only person seated on one of those tables was a girl who was totally engrossed in the book she was reading. Her nose was buried in the book which was blocking her face from my view.

I walked over and chose a seat at the corner table on the other side of that open sitting area.

"No chance I can make it now," I murmured to myself, glancing at my watch which showed that it was already 10:00 p.m. It only made sense that I cancelled my flight.

I knew before coming to Darjeeling that there were multiple flights which operate from Bagdogra to Mumbai during morning hours. But looking at the jam, I thought it would be wiser to purchase a ticket directly from the airline ticket counter once I reached the airport.

"Sir, what can I get you?" A young boy wearing a thick woollen sweater with a muffler wrapped around his neck came and asked.

"Do you have a menu card?" I asked

"No menu card sir, but we have eggs, Maggi, momos, sandwiches, tea and coffee at this hour."

"Momos sound good, especially in this weather," I replied.

"Yes sir, my mom makes very tasty momos. You will love them."

"Is it?" I smiled at the boy.

"Yes sir," he happily praised his mom's culinary skill.

"Ok then! Please get me some hot momos and a cup of tea after that."

"Sure sir." The boy took the order and went inside again.

It was fairly cold since the place was located in between a cluster of hills. Starting to feel the chill, I pulled on the jacket I was carrying and zipped it up till my neck. Stuck with nothing to do, I thought I would call a few people. But the network was pretty poor.

"Damn!" I was getting frustrated now.

I had so many things that needed to be done. My phone wasn't working and it was pointless to open the laptop since there was no internet connectivity.

I glanced at the girl who was sitting in the corner, still busy reading her book.

I wondered if I should walk up to her and ask if I could use her cell phone to make just one call if there was network on her cell phone.

'Nah!' I thought to myself. 'I'd probably look very silly asking for her phone.'

But that one call was important as I had a few meetings lined up for the next morning, which needed to be rescheduled. I finally decided to approach her.

She still appeared quite lost in her book as I walked towards her.

"Excuse me," I said

"Yes," she replied, turning towards me.

Beautiful! One glance at her and I was lost in her beauty. She had a magnificent face with attractive eyes, which would catch anyone's attention. Deep but bright eyes, perfectly-shaped lips and flowing curly hair till above her shoulder gave her a perfect look. She was beautiful enough to charm anyone with her beauty.

"Can I help you?" she said, this time a bit louder.

Gosh! I was actually checking her out.

"Sorry, sorry to disturb you ma'am, but..."

"But what?" she asked before I could finish my sentence.

"Ma'am, actually I was wondering if your cell phone has network connectivity."

"Why?"

"I need to make an important call."

"What about your phone?" she asked pointing to my cell phone, which was clutched in my hand.

"There is no network," I said, showing her my phone display. "I just need to make one call, ma'am. It's really urgent."

"I am sorry, but why don't you use the restaurant's phone?" she said pointing towards the counter which had a landline.

"You don't trust me?" I asked.

"I don't know you, mister. Forget about trusting you. Please use that phone." She pointed at the counter phone and went back to reading her book.

"I understand, ma'am. That's perfectly okay. I will try that phone," I said politely.

Well, she was definitely strange. Strange, but right! How can she trust me? What a fool I was to ask her that. I walked towards the counter.

Luckily, the phone was working and I could manage a quick call and have my meetings postponed. I then returned to my table. It was best to avoid any further interaction with the girl. She is very blunt and straightforward, I thought.

"Thanks," I said as the boy came with the order and placed a plate of piping hot momos and tea in front of me.

While taking a sip of the hot tea, I glanced at her once again and realized that she was still lost in her book.

There was something enigmatic about that girl sitting all alone, not having anyone with her. It was kind of strange. I thought for a while. For some reason, I got up from my table and started walking towards hcr.

"Excuse me," I said holding the plate of momos in one hand and tea in the other one.

"I told you there is a phone which you can use," she said, getting irritated this time.

"I know, I know, ma'am. Thank you. I was able to make the call," I said, keeping the plate on the table while I was still standing. "Actually, I thought maybe we can sit together. It looks like we are in for a long night. And it would probably be better if we both kept each other company just to kill the time," I replied pointing at the long queue of vehicles.

"I have my own way to kill my time," she replied showing me the thick book she was reading.

"I see, but do you mind if I sit here and have my snacks? I don't like to sit alone," I replied, making a face.

"I am sorry but I don't know you, and I don't prefer to talk with strangers." She probably thought it was best to be brutally honest this time.

"Well, if I introduced myself, then we wouldn't be strangers, would we?" I said smiling at her. "My name is Kabir and you are...?"

She did not respond. Instead, she just kept looking at me.

'Gosh!' I thought. 'She really has beautiful eyes.'

"Trust me, ma'am. I do not have any intention to disturb you. It's just that we all are stuck here. When I saw you sitting alone, I couldn't resist coming and talking with you. I thought we could both use the company."

Again, she chose not to respond.

"If you aren't comfortable or if you think I am disturbing you, then I shall leave you alone with your book," I said and turned to leave.

I don't know why, but I really wanted to get to know her. There was just something magnetic about this beautiful girl sitting absolutely alone, away from the rest of the world. That seemed to captivate me.

"I am Anamika," she said.

I turned back as I heard her whisper

"What?"

"I said my name is Anamika," she said, looking at me.

"Oh, that's a nice name," I replied. "Would it be alright if I join you?" I asked, pointing at the chair.

She nodded her head and kept the book aside.

"Thanks, Anamika. Momos?" I offered.

"No, thank you."

"They are hot and really tasty. I am sure you will like them," I said, trying to tempt her.

"I said no!" Her response was firm.

"As you wish," I muttered and stuffed another hot momo into my mouth. "So, what do you do Anamika?"

"Nothing."

"Nothing? You don't like look like a student, so I am sure you must be working somewhere, right?"

"I don't work anywhere. I just breathe in life."

"Breathe in your life! And how does one do that?" I asked.

"I travel to a lot of places, cities and countries. I love books and read a lot. I believe in following the rhythm of my heart and do what I feel like in the moment. I connect with myself and that's how I breathe in life."

"Wow, sounds good. And you do all of this alone?"

"Yes, absolutely alone. Only when you are alone, you can connect with your soul. With others, you have to pretend to be someone you're not. You can never really show the other person your true self."

"Quite philosophical!" I responded. "So, where all have you travelled?"

"Wherever there is peace," she quickly responded.

"Peace? Well, that's a big word. So, where did you last travel?" I asked.

"Darjeeling, of course," she replied.

"Oh, it's a very beautiful place, with its pristine mountains, lakes—"

"I didn't come here as a tourist to explore the city," Anamika clarified.

"Then?"

"I came here to spend my time at a monastery."

"Monastery? What did you do there?"

"Nothing, I just relaxed, listened to my heartbeat, disconnected with the outer world and was able to connect with the world inside me," she explained calmly.

"Earlier you seemed philosophical. Now, you're spiritual. I am impressed, Ms Anamika."

I was trying to make sense of what she was saying. "So, what do you get out of all this? I mean, you travel the world alone, do what you like and visit peaceful places. You must be looking for something? What is it?"

Taking a deep breath and looking towards the open sky, she replied, "I am searching for myself."

That was once again a mysterious answer which didn't help me gain any insight about her at all. "Do you feel you have lost yourself somewhere?" I asked, getting a bit curious.

She did not respond, but kept looking away.

"Hellooo," I said loudly, trying to draw her attention back. "Is everything ok?" I asked.

"Yes, all good," she replied softly.

Now, I was convinced that she had a story to share, but what was it? I was falling for the charisma of this charming and mysterious girl. I couldn't wait to know more.

"Where are you from, Anamika?" I enquired.

"You ask too many questions, Kabir."

"Because you don't answer." Our eyes met.

"I don't like to be questioned," she replied after a few seconds.

"And I like to find the answers to everything going around me."

It felt like we both were going in circles. She wanted to escape the conversation and I wasn't letting her do that.

"Why don't you tell me something about yourself?" she asked.

"Good move in shifting the conversation to me," I said, smiling. "But that's ok. Ask me what you want to know."

"Everything, what's your story?" she asked.

"Ha ha ha! Well, that's very simple because I don't have a great story. Still, I will tell you something about me. But first, some coffee?" I asked

"Sure."

# 3

## *Kabir*

"You did it, Kabir!" I told myself as soon as I reached the 27th floor of the Escalate Towers in Worli, Mumbai. It was my first day at work. I wore a grey non-branded suit which I had bought specifically to wear during my job interviews during the last semester of my MBA days in Mumbai. I got my shoes stitched and polished from the cobbler outside my paying guest accommodation at Mira Road, which was the other end of the city. The deodorant helped beat the remnants of the local train ride to work. The smell of humankind is not always pleasant.

I was inevitably reminded of my mother, who had started working shortly after dad's unexpected death. Our so-called well-wishers turned away. Dad didn't have a lot of savings apart from our home in Manali. So, after his death, we had to make do with the money we received from the pension. With time, compromising became an important part of our DNA. The only place mom ensured that we did not compromise was on my education. She was confident that armed with a good education, we could come out of this situation.

She could not have been more correct. I focused on my education and year after year, I worked really hard to get into the best colleges. Thanks to my grades, I received a scholarship in a well-known MBA college in Mumbai. That's how my journey in Mumbai started.

Leaving Maa alone in Manali to come to Mumbai was a difficult decision for us. But we both knew that this was our only option to make our condition better.

I remembered how in Mumbai, along with my studies, I used to work part-time in the evening at an international call centre to support my expenses. Though the job was part-time, the money I earned was sufficient to defray my expenses in Mumbai.

The initial months were really difficult. The climate, the food and most importantly, travelling by local trains – all of it needed major adjustments.

The local trains are the lifeline of Mumbai. You can look forward to full body massages the rest of the travellers insist on giving you. I was sometimes left thinking that I would be crushed to death. The worst part was getting on and off the train. It was easier to just go with the flow as fighting the stream of people just made everything more difficult. For someone like me, who came from a place where your personal space was actually personal in reality, it was tough getting used to this strange city.

Despite all these obstacles, what kept me going was the hunger to prove myself. I worked hard consistently and kept my focus on the goal. Soon, Mumbai accepted me just like it does to thousands of people who come there every single day. The only thing that kept me motivated till the end was the dream of making a successful career so that whatever hardships Maa had gone through in the past would all be replaced with eternal happiness in the future.

With my admission in a good college, a part-time job and the company of innumerable unknown Mumbaikars around me, I didn't realize how quickly, the two years of MBA got over.

Today, I was sitting at the Escalate Towers to meet the MD of Blenks International Media house, one of key advertising players in the market.

"Sir," a female voice drew my attention.

"Yes?" I stood up.

"Mr Taneja will meet you in his cabin."

"Sure," I said confidently.

"This way please," said the cute old lady. Out of nervousness, I adjusted my tie one more time before entering the cabin.

"May I come in, sir?" I asked.

"Come in," he answered.

I entered Mr Taneja's huge cabin. Mr Taneja, MD of Blenks International Media, was in his late forties or maybe early fifties. He was a short, bald guy wearing a suit. He had a cigar in his hand and was busy looking out at the skyscrapers from behind the huge glass window of his cabin.

I stood silently, nervously waiting for him to acknowledge my presence.

"These skyscrapers have already reached the sky. Who knows where it will end," he said, turning towards me.

"Good morning, sir," I greeted him. He only nodded.

"Mumbai, sir. Due to lack of space, these skyscrapers are coming up everywhere. It seems like everyone wants to reach the sky."

"Exactly! Just like these skyscrapers, the competition among young professionals like you has been reaching far with every passing day. If you want to get ahead of the curve, you will have to ensure that you are seated on top of everyone," he said pointing at one of the tallest skyscrapers.

"I understand, sir."

"Good! I am sure you have lots of potential Kabir, which is why my team has chosen you. It's time for you to put your best foot forward, show your calibre and creativity to our clients to grow with us."

"I will, sir," I acknowledged.

"Trust me, Kabir. If you do that, we will ensure that you reach great heights of success. We will fulfil every dream you came to Mumbai with."

"I am here to make a mark for myself. I will ensure that I leave a mark with my hard work and dedication."

"Welcome onboard, Kabir," he said and extended his hand for a handshake.

"My secretary Freny will guide you to your workstation and will introduce you to other team members," he said, lighting his cigar.

"Thank you, sir."

Freny, Mr Taneja's old but cute secretary escorted me to my workstation.

"Guys, meet Kabir! He's your new team member," Freny said, introducing me to a few people who were huddled together to look at something on a laptop.

"Hi, everyone," I greeted everyone.

"Meet Shruti, she is in the same team as you," Freny said, gesturing to one of the girls.

"And this is Mohit. He is the creative director of Blenks International. You will be reporting to him."

"Hello, sir!" I greeted Mohit.

"Mohit. Everybody here calls me Mohit".

"Sure, Mohit."

"Okay then, enjoy your day. In case you need anything, please feel free to ask me," Freny said.

I thanked her before she walked back to her desk.

For the rest of the day, I was subjected to a more detailed introduction session with my team members. I spent time understanding the role and responsibilities better.

Mohit was an old employee at BIM and he had pulled himself up to the ranks through his determination and will power. He had worked really hard to earn his current position. Shruti had joined BIM a few months back. She was assisting Mohit on various advertising campaigns. This was her first assignment.

Shruti had shifted to Mumbai from Ajmer in Rajasthan. She lived with a friend in a paying guest accommodation. She was a typical small town beautiful girl from Rajasthan who had a dream of living life on her own terms and conditions.

Mohit was born and brought up in Mumbai. He had started working at BIM nine years back as an Associate Innovator, just like me. Slowly and gradually, his work got noticed, elevating him up the ranks. He was a motivation for others like me.

I was happy that finally my career had begun and I was associated with such talented people. It was now my turn to learn and make a mark for myself.

Days passed and I started enjoying my assignments. The job was very demanding, hence with every new client, I had to come up with unique ideas as everyone wanted a different advertisement campaign. I started learning the tricks of the trade and within no time, I started gaining popularity.

It had been one year and Maa was happy that things were smooth. I had met her when I took a Diwali break. I had asked her to come and stay with me in Mumbai but she was happy in

Manali. The finances at home were now taken care of and our life ahead seemed good.

Mumbai was really turning things around for me. I was thoroughly enjoying my journey in the city of dreams. But I was still waiting for my dreams to turn into reality.

And as they say nowadays, opportunity doesn't knock your door, it rings.

# 4

That one fine night, when I was busy dreaming about a great life in Mumbai, my cell phone rang at 2:30 a.m.

"Shruti? So late?" I felt worried. "Is everything okay?"

"Kabir, we have a problem," she said. "I just got a call. Mohit has met with an accident. He has been admitted in the hospital."

"What? How did this happen?" I said, getting up from my bed.

"He was driving back from Pune this evening and he met with an accident on the Mumbai - Pune expressway," she said and started crying.

"Oh my god, hope there are no major injuries?"

"Listen, I don't know about his medical condition. I have called you regarding the Sky Leads presentation tomorrow. Mohit was supposed to present the campaign to their top management tomorrow. Do you remember?"

Sky Leads was the overseas real estate player that was entering the Mumbai real estate market. How could I not remember it!

All of us had been working day and night on this big deal and Mohit was supposed to present the campaign to the management. Keeping in mind the benefits out of this deal, our team was assigned the task of preparing a proposal which had to be so good that they couldn't refuse.

"I remember. I think we will have to postpone tomorrow's meeting," I said

"No, we can't. The clients have already reached Mumbai from overseas and at this point of time, we cannot postpone it," she replied. "Plus, we don't know what Mohit's condition is like."

"I get it, but even now, he isn't in a condition to present the idea. Who else could possibly make the presentation in his place?" I asked.

"You, Kabir."

"Me?" I was shocked. "Are you out of your mind, Shruti? I have never made a presentation to any of the clients on my own. I might goof up things. And you also know how critical these clients are."

"I know, but Mr Taneja is determined to close this deal and has demanded you to handle tomorrow's meeting."

"But Shruti, what if I goof up?"

"And what if you don't, Kabir?" she said in a calm tone this time. "You have to handle this. Taneja believes in you and this is your opportunity to prove your worth. You have been working closely on this with Mohit. I am sure you will be able to handle it."

"I am not sure if I can."

"Give it a shot, Kabir! We don't have any other option. This project is a big deal for the company and you still have a few hours to prepare. Just go through each and every detail of the project and you will be fine," she assured.

"Let me try," I said, looking at the clock. It was 2:45 a.m. and the meeting was at 9:30 a.m.

"All the best, Kabir. I will see you directly in the office," Shruti said, before hanging up.

"God, why me?" I said, throwing my phone on the bed.

"Come on, Kabir. Don't be nervous. Prepare yourself," my inner voice boosted me up.

I prepared a cup of coffee and started to read through the details of the campaign and proposal. In a few of hours, I had gone through all the important aspects of the presentation and prepared some key highlights to pitch to the clients.

I looked at the clock when I was done. It was 6:30 a.m. I took a hot shower and got ready. For a change, I caught a cab to reach the office to face the clients.

"All the best, Kabir," Freny said as I walked towards the board room.

"Thanks, Freny. I hope he does not fire me after this," I said, pointing at Taneja's cabin.

"Ha ha! Don't worry. You will rock." She winked.

I entered the board room. The presentation, followed by a discussion, continued for almost five hours. Shruti was there to support me wherever I felt I needed help. Post the meeting, Taneja took the clients out for lunch and we decided to go and meet Mohit.

Mohit was still under observation because of multiple fractures. He had a lot of stitches on his face. No one was allowed to meet him. I met his family and offered my help and support. There was nothing much we could do at the hospital hence, Shruti and I decided to go back home.

By the time I reached home, it was evening. I was exhausted. I chose to have an early dinner and dozed off almost immediately.

"Mr Taneja wants to see you in his cabin," Freny told me over the office intercom the next morning while I was busy checking my emails.

"Me? Why?" I asked.

"I don't know, but come quickly," she answered.

'Oh god! I think I must have goofed up yesterday.' I thought as I recollected the previous day's presentation and discussion.

I adjusted my tie and started walking towards his cabin. My hands were starting to sweat and I was almost trembling.

Once inside the cabin, I could not read the boss's expression at all. He asked me, "Kabir, do you know what you did in yesterday's presentation?" he asked, coming to the topic directly.

My throat choked. I could feel my body going numb with shock and fear.

"What, sir?" I asked softly.

"The clients," he stopped to light up the cigar.

"The clients shared their feedback, sir?" I asked.

"Yes," he replied.

"What did they have to say, sir?" I asked, my heart, in my mouth.

"You knew how critical this deal was for us, didn't you?" He asked, looking straight into my eyes. His tone changed.

"Yes, sir." His serious expression told me that I had mucked things up yesterday.

"You did a wonderful job, Kabir!" he said loudly.

"What?" I was surprised.

"Yes, Kabir. I just received an email from the client, appreciating your proposal and agreeing to our terms and conditions, except one."

"What is that?" I asked.

"They want you to lead this entire campaign for them, right from the beginning till the end. They have clearly mentioned the same in their email," he said, pointing to his laptop screen.

"What? Me?" I was surprised because one need years of experience to lead an entire campaign. This had always been the case at BIM and I had only one year of experience under my belt.

"But sir, how can I lead this project?".

"Why not! You delivered a wonderful presentation yesterday. The clients liked the proposal and they want *you* to work on this with them. Then, why not?" He spoke.

"But sir, this was supposed to be led by Mohit."

"I know, Kabir. But I went to see Mohit yesterday and the doctors said he will still take at least two months to get back to work. You know we can't afford to lose this project, right? This is a great opportunity for both you and our company."

Mr Taneja got up and paced around the room. His eyes pierced through me.

"Trust me, once you complete this campaign, you will move far ahead from your colleagues. You will be living your dream. It's up to you to turn it into reality or let it remain a dream," he said, looking straight into my eyes and hoping to hear a 'yes' from me.

"I am ready, sir," I replied instantly.

"Good then. I am very happy with your performance and have decided to give you a straight 30% raise and a lucrative bonus."

30%! I was shocked.

"You deserve it, my boy. I have organized a small party at my place tonight. You are warmly invited so be there. Freny will share the details with you."

"Thank you very much, sir. I am really thankful."

"See you tonight," he said.

"Yes!" I shouted as soon as I came out of his cabin.

I reached my desk and looked outside the glass window. I was happy at my first achievement. This was a stepping stone to my success.

I was looking forward to the party in the evening, unaware of the fact that a beautiful hurricane was waiting for me there.

# 5

Shruti and I reached Taneja's penthouse in the posh suburb of Bandra. Besides us, there were also a few other office colleagues. Taneja had invited a few of our current clients as well. There were a couple of more guests, who I believe, were his friends.

When we arrived, some of the guests were talking, some were dancing, while a few had chosen to lounge around and observe the antics. The remaining ones were holding a drink in their hand, standing next to the live barbeque at the terrace.

"There he is, the man of the hour!" Taneja said walking towards us.

"Good evening, sir." We both wished him.

"A very good evening indeed, Kabir." Then, Mr Taneja turned to look at a beautiful and elegant woman. "Honey, meet Kabir. Remember, I told you about him? He's the reason for tonight's party."

I was wondering who she was when I was told, "And Kabir, meet my wife Yamini."

Wife! Shruti and I were shocked, but we managed to control our emotions. Yamini looked much younger than Taneja. She had this sheer elegance about her. She was beautiful, with fair skin and sharp features. The gown she wore showcased her perfect figure. Though she was older than the other girls around, she was the prettiest of them all.

"Hi Kabir," she greeted me sweetly.

"Hello ma'am," I wished back.

Shruti only nodded in response. I guess she did not like the way Mr Taneja had introduced Yamini only to me and not to her.

"Mr Taneja told me how you stole our clients' hearts and managed to grab this deal all alone," Yamini said.

"Thanks, ma'am. It was all team work. And, sir has been extremely generous with his praise."

"He and generous! No way, Kabir. He is a businessman. He only invests where he can see clear returns," she said and laughed.

Shruti looked at me and realized that we also had to laugh at her comment.

"Business runs on returns and profits, honey. That's how I have managed to create this small empire," he said, lighting his cigar.

"And I am proud of you, darling," Yamini quickly responded.

"Why don't you guys get yourself a drink? We will go and meet some of our other guests," Mr Taneja said.

"Sure sir," Shruti replied.

"Enjoy the party," Mr Taneja said.

"See you guys, have fun!" Yamini said as they walked away to attend to other guests.

As they both left, Shruti and I made ourselves comfortable at the bar counter.

"Looks like Taneja is really impressed with your work," Shruti said, sipping her drink.

"Yup, I guess so. Why else would he mention me to his wife?" I said.

"Yeah! But look at his wife, Kabir. How could she marry an oldie like Taneja?"

"True, she is much younger," I said.

"Money matters, Kabir."

"I guess so, but it's none of our business," I said, sipping my drink.

We both were having a good time. Shruti had to leave the party after a while as her flatmate was not keeping well and she needed to take her to the doctor. I wanted to go along with her, but she insisted that I stay there as Mr Taneja may not like it. So, reluctantly, I chose to stay back.

I simply stood in a corner at the party, enjoying the beautiful view of Bandra Worli sea link from the balcony, holding a drink in my hand. I was reflecting on what all this city had given me in just one year. For someone like me, it was truly an achievement. Finally, I was enjoying my so-called little success today.

"Enjoying the view?" I looked back. It was Yamini.

"Yes ma'am; it's beautiful," I said.

"Hmm. The air is also so fresh here. I spend most of my time here at night," Yamini said.

I smiled. It was indeed a fabulous place to be.

"So, tell me about yourself Kabir, if you don't mind?" she asked.

I told her about myself, my small family and how my mother brought me up with limited resources. I told her about my scholarship, coming to Mumbai, and how I used to work part-time to support my studies. She kept listening to me without any interruption. I said everything as honestly as I could. After all, someone was listening to me for the first time.

"Wow, it's really good to see that your mother's sacrifices and your hard work are finally paying off," she said, sweetly. "Not many people are able to convert obstacles into opportunities. I am happy you did it, Kabir."

"Thank you, ma'am."

"Where do you live in Mumbai, Kabir?"

"Mira Road. I have rented an apartment which I share with a friend," I answered

"Oh, it must be very exhausting travelling from Mira Road to the office every day. They are practically located at two opposite ends of Mumbai."

"I am now used to it, ma'am. I have been living there since my MBA days."

"College days were different, Kabir. Now you are a professional. You have a successful career and you are doing well financially. Then, why take so much of travel pain? Shift somewhere closer to the office," she advised.

"The house rent in this side of the city is very high," I said, looking at the other tall buildings around.

"Oh Kabir, now that you have moved up in your career, you need to stop thinking about these small costs. Think big.Think of how you could productively utilize the time you save if you shift closer to the office," she said.

"But..."

"What's happening, guys?" Taneja said as he walked towards us.

"Honey, I was telling Kabir that he should shift somewhere closer to our office so that he can save time on travel. It will ultimately help him in concentrating on his current projects."

"Ma'am, I will manage," I replied.

Taneja looked at me and Yamini for a while. "Yamini is right, Kabir. I have a suggestion," he thought for a while and said.

We both looked at him.

"We have a small apartment here in Bandra, which we had bought purely for investment purposes. It's been years, but no one lives there. Why don't you move in there? This will solve all your travelling issues," he suggested.

Apartment in Bandra? Was I dreaming? Someone, pinch me please!

"But sir, I don't think I can afford it," I replied.

"Don't worry about it. You can pay me a slightly higher rent than what you are paying currently. But in return, you work hard for me and get me more such deals." He beamed.

Yamini looked at me, smiling at Taneja's suggestion.

"Remember, I told you I am a true businessman," he laughed as he responded to me.

"Thank you so much for this kind gesture, sir," I said to him.

"Don't thank me. Thank her if you want to," he said, looking at Yamini.

"Thanks a lot, ma'am."

"Work hard for this company, Kabir, and I am sure you will reach new heights of success soon," Taneja cheered.

"Cheers!" she said, raising her glass.

# 6

I shifted to the apartment in Bandra soon after, and my life changed.

Bandra has its own lifestyle – it is less crowded, but always happening. With beautiful churches around at almost all the corners, you can feel positivity in the air. With Bollywood celebrities' houses around and beautiful sunsets before my eyes, Bandra was a different experience for me.

Maa also visited Mumbai once after I shifted to the new house. She was very happy with the kind of progress I had made. I asked her to stay with me but she turned me down saying Mumbai was too fast-paced for her.

Life looked like a dream. Along with the new designation came a lot of perks too. From a guy who used to travel in local trains, I was now someone who drove a BMW!

With time, I lost more of myself to the corporate lifestyle. I was working all the time, constantly attending meetings, managing clients and getting the deals closed. I was happy about this life initially, but deep down, I knew this was not going to last forever. Moreover, I didn't want to constantly look for opportunities to crack deals. Rather, I wanted to spend time understanding the real meaning of life. I wanted to write stories that would reach out to people and positively impact their lives.

Right from my childhood, I had a keen interest in writing. I wanted to take it up as a career but because of our financial condition, I couldn't do that. And now, when I had everything I didn't have time to take it up as I was too focused on my career.

♡

It was Mr and Mrs Taneja's wedding anniversary and I was invited to the party. Shruti had gone to Ajmer to see her parents over the weekend, so I was all by myself.

"I would like to wish you both a very happy anniversary," I said and handed over a beautiful flower bouquet to the couple.

"Thanks, Kabir," Mr Taneja replied.

"You are looking beautiful, ma'am," I said.

"Thank you, Kabir," she replied.

"You know, Yamini! Once again he has proved that he is the rock star of our company. The recent deal will indeed make our competitors cry. He has managed to snatch the deal from right under their noses," he said and laughed.

"I am trying hard to prove myself, sir. I want to be like you," I said, trying to soothe his ego.

"I am sure with the kind of talent you have and the hard work you are putting in, you are not very far from your target," Mr Taneja said, sipping the scotch in his hand.

"Thank you, sir. Whatever I am today, it's only because you gave me a chance. I owe my success to you both, for giving me the job I love and the house I am so thankful for," I said, looking at her.

"Oh, that was nothing, Kabir. It was just an empty house," she said.

"That empty house became my home, ma'am," I replied. Yamini looked at me for a while.

"Nice! Now I know why our clients are impressed with you. You have a spark in you, Kabir," Yamini said.

She kept looking at me constantly, which made me conscious.

"Hi, Mr Gupta," Mr Taneja said, waving at one of our clients. "Excuse me, I will be back in a while," he said and walked away.

Now, it was just me and Yamini, standing next to each other. I don't know why, but her eyes were constantly on me and I was getting conscious.

"So, now that you have some spare time with you, what else do you do apart from work, Kabir?" she asked, taking a sip from her drink.

"Nothing much! I hardly get time to do anything. Your husband keeps me busy all the time," I said pointing at Mr Taneja.

"He is a workaholic; his priorities are different. For him, work comes first," she said looking at him.

"That's how he has created this company. He has achieved everything on his own," I replied

"That's true, but you are still young and have your whole life in front of you," she said.

"So, what should I do?" I asked, not knowing where she was headed with the conversation.

"Enjoy your life, Kabir! Not many who come to Mumbai achieve so much at your age. They struggle and have no time to spend on the things they love doing," she said. "You are lucky that you have everything at this age. Go out, make friends, socialize, work hard and party harder. You should not have any regrets in life," she said.

She was right.

"Don't you have a girl in your life?" she asked a more personal question now.

"No way, ma'am," I replied

"Why?"

"Never felt that way about anyone. Rather, I did not have time to notice anyone," I answered her.

"I understand, but now that you've achieved your goal, what's stopping you from finding the right girl? You really need someone in your life, Kabir. Life is all about love and companionship." She almost pouted and said, "And the real meaning of enjoyment... you know what I mean?"

I looked at her and presumed that she was pulling my leg. But she was smiling at me in a manner that made me nervous.

"So, what's the discussion on?" Mr Taneja was back.

"Nothing, honey. I was telling Kabir that now since he has everything, why doesn't he settle down." She managed to twist the conversation pretty well.

"Please don't ruin his life," he commented.

She didn't reply but kept looking at me. In that moment, I noticed a different Yamini for the first time.

"Yes Maa, I will come home this Diwali. I promise," I told my mother over our Sunday phone call.

"That's what you told me before Holi as well. You got busy with some work at the last moment and did not turn up," she replied, showing anger.

She was right. I often made promises to visit her, but couldn't fulfill them.

"This time, I promise you, I will book my tickets right now," I said, assuring her.

"I will see," she said in a dull voice.

"Oh c'mon, Maa! When I come home this time, I will also make sure that you come back with me to Mumbai," I said.

"No, thank you. I am happy here in Manali. I will never get used to Mumbai."

"But Maa, Mumbai is amazing."

"For you, yes! For your Maa, Manali is perfect. This house reminds me of the good times I shared with your dad. I can't leave it."

"Okay Maa, you win, I lose," I said.

The doorbell rang while I was talking to her. I bade her goodbye and rushed to open the door. The doorbell rang constantly all this while.

I opened the door and was surprised to see Yamini at the door.

"Oh, hello ma'am."

"Hi, Kabir."

"Wow, what a surprise!" I said, looking at her. I was surprised to see her at my place on a Sunday morning.

"Can I walk into my own house or do we continue this conversation while I stand at the door? she taunted.

"I am really sorry, ma'am. Please come in," I said, making way for her to enter.

"Hmm, I must say that you have kept the house very neat and clean. I thought it would be a messy bachelor's pad," she said, taking a quick glance around the apartment.

"I can't stand if the house is not spick and span all the time, ma'am."

"Oh stop calling me ma'am, Kabir. How many times have I told you to call me by my name. I have such a beautiful name, isn't it?" she said, making herself comfortable on the couch.

"Yes, it is... Yamini," I said, getting a bit nervous.

"Come, sit here! Why are you still standing?" she said, patting the seat right next to her.

"Thanks," I said and walked over to the other end of the couch.

"Nervous?" she asked me.

"Hmm, not really," I answered, trying to hide the fact that I was actually freaking out.

What was I supposed to do in a situation like this! Firstly, the apartment belonged to my boss and he was generously letting me stay here. Secondly, on a Sunday morning, my boss's hot wife was visiting me for the first time. And while we both were alone in the apartment, she also happened to be checking me out.

"So, tell me, did you consider the advice I gave you the last time we met?"

"What are you talking about?"

"About enjoying your life."

"Oh that, yes! I mean no, Yamini. Nothing has changed in my life. Office, work, meetings and clients continue to be an integral part of my life," I replied.

"Oh, poor Kabir," she came near me and placed her hand on my lap, which made me very uncomfortable.

"Where is sir today?" I asked, just to change the topic.

"As usual, busy meeting some client," she replied in a tone that showed her disinterest in this line of conversation.

"Client meeting today? But it's a Sunday!" I asked, surprised.

"For him, all the days are the same. I told you he is a workaholic whose only priority is his work and no one else," she continued in a dull tone.

I chose to keep quiet. She was talking about a workaholic who was paying me a very high salary every month.

"You know what Kabir, he hardly has time for me. He has time for everything – for work, for meetings, for foreign tours, everything. But not me," she said, sounding upset.

"He is working hard to give you everything you want in life, Yamini. He wants to make you happy."

"Happy! Do you think happiness comes from all these materialistic things? No Kabir!" she continued. "Happiness means spending time together with your loved ones, having a conversation with them, being there for each other all the time, laughing together and listening to what the other person has to say. Happiness does not mean sharing the same bed but sleeping on the edges. And if that isn't enough, then sleeping alone most of the time, waiting for him to come back home," Yamini concluded.

I was shocked by Yamini's last outburst. I was beginning to understand the situation she was in. The loneliness in her life was the reason she was here.

"Kabir, this is why I told you to enjoy your life. To do what you like doing and not just run after your career with a tunnel vision." She let out a deep sigh before saying, "I know you are very talented, Kabir. You have a successful career ahead of you, but at the same time, I can also see that behind this talented and hard-working person is an innocent guy, who believes in enjoying each and every moment of his life," she said.

"Don't let that real Kabir die inside you. Live your life, spread happiness, do what makes you happy, even if it looks stupid to others," she looked into my eyes and concluded.

Her words hit my heart somewhere. In pursuit of happiness, we all choose to run the rat race, but never realise that happiness comes from within. I guess we need to find ourselves first and then, the rest will follow.

She came closer to me, "Can I ask you for a favour?"

I didn't know what she was going to ask and I wasn't sure if I wanted to know either.

I could feel her breath now as we were that close. "Tell me."

"Can you help me come out of this loneliness?" Yamini said and kissed my neck.

"What are you doing Yamini?" I said and pushed her back.

"Doing what I think is right since the first time I saw you, Kabir."

"Please stop it!" I said, trying to avoid eye contact with her.

"Why Kabir? Am I not beautiful? Look at me, Kabir!" she said and pulled the zipper of her jacket down to lure me with her curves.

"I said stop it Yamini! I am not what you think." I yelled now.

"Oh, but what about that hunger to reach the sky that I noticed the first time we met?" I looked at her, confused and appalled. "I can help you with whatever you want Kabir – an amazing career, promotion, perks, anything you say."

"Trust me, no one would come to know about this. I have been lonely for so long, but didn't dare to approach anyone. With you, I feel different. Please help me in ending this loneliness," she almost pleaded this time.

Yamini came in front of my eyes. For the first time, I saw what she must be going through. She was not luring me; she was badly in need of companionship and comfort.

"Of course I am hungry for success, Yamini, but that doesn't mean I would use such an unethical way to reach there," I said clearly.

"Do you even know what you are talking about? This can cost you your career!"

I looked at her and replied after some thought, "I have nothing to lose. I can live without a great career but cannot live with the fact that I compromised my ethics and used a woman's loneliness to climb the ladder of success."

I could see that Yamini wasn't expecting a rejection. She was shocked. As far as I was concerned, I knew I was taking a big chance. She could get me fired the next day by putting allegations on me, but I was prepared to face it. She had given me a home, her husband was someone who had trusted me and gave me a successful career that I had always dreamed of. How could I spoil everything!

"Look Yamini, you have issues and you are lonely, but there are other ways to deal with it. And one such way is to have a friend like me in your life," I said.

"Friend?" Yamini asked.

"Yeah! I understand your loneliness, but you are not like other desperate women who choose to cheat on their husbands. You have a kind heart, Yamini. You care for others. It's just that time isn't on your side."

I made her understand and passed a glass of water to her. She took a couple of sips and calmed down.

"All you need is a true friend who can help you come out of this loneliness. And, I am here. Ready to be that friend," I said and got up from the couch to wipe Yamini's tears.

"Thanks for this, Kabir. You are right. I am glad that I have found a friend in you," she said and hugged me.

There was complete silence between us. All Yamini needed was someone by her side whom she could trust with her true feelings. At that moment I learnt a very important lesson. It is not money, it is not luxury, it is not the best of everything in life which can give happiness. Rather, it's the company of someone with whom you can talk with, smile and share your feelings with. It is in these blissful moments where true happiness lies.

For the first time I realized that Mr Taneja was a poor man. He was running behind money, leaving the real treasure behind.

Once Yamini left, I picked up my phone and dialled Maa's number. "Maa, keep the laddus ready. I am coming home this Diwali."

# 7

## Darjeeling highway

Kabir had just finished narrating his story.

"Wow! That is very interesting and inspirational," Anamika said, finishing her second coffee.

"Really? I know it's interesting, but what's so inspirational about it?" I asked, rubbing my hands together. The temperature had dropped further.

"For a guy like you, who has seen so much of struggle in life, it is incredible to see how you are able to finally overcome all the challenges and achieve this kind of success," Anamika said.

"Thanks."

"And yes, I feel sad about Yamini," Anamika said.

"Yes, me too."

"She puts on a brave face for the world and pretends to be happy. But on the inside, she is just a lonely woman, desperate for some love, affection and attention. It's difficult. I think each one of us has two different sides – one that we keep to ourselves, and the other that we choose to display to the world," Anamika said, taking a deep breath.

"True," I said.

We both sat quietly, looking at the valley, probably thinking about the life we were living.

"So, what's your story?" I asked after a while.

"I told you, Kabir. I really don't have anything to share," she replied.

"I am sure you do. I can see that in your eyes," I said.

"Oh, my eyes!" she said, maintaining the eye contact with me.

"You just agreed that we all have two different sides to ourselves. What if the one that the world sees is not real?" she asked.

"Then, tell me who the real Anamika is," I said softly, coaxing her.

"It would not be that easy," she replied.

"Life has been tough on me as well," I said.

"Hmm, are you sure you want to listen to my side of the story?" she asked.

"Of course. Can't turn back now. I have told you everything about me," I said

"I know, but not everyone has a bright story. At times, it's dark and it changes a person's life completely." Anamika got up from her place and walked towards the wooden fencing at the edge of the open hall. I followed her.

"What do you mean?" I asked.

"Nothing."

"Tell me, Anamika," I insisted

"It's a hurricane of emotions that I have been carrying inside me all these years. It is not that easy to spill it, Kabir," she replied, turning towards me.

"Sometimes, it is good to let that hurricane out. I am sure you will feel much better," I assured her.

"But why with you?"

I smiled. "Because we don't know each other and I will not judge you as a person. There will be no right or wrong, so go ahead," I said.

"On one condition," she said, after thinking for a while.

"And what is that?"

"Once I finish my story, you will not ask anything further. Once this night is over, we will get back to our lives, to our respective worlds. There will be no contact, no further communication at all. Most importantly, you will not look for me anywhere," she said.

"But Anamika..."

"Kabir, this is the only condition on which I will share my story."

"You are very stubborn, Anamika. But ok, I will try," I replied.

"I hope our paths never cross again and we don't meet after this, Kabir."

"You never know, Anamika. For now, let's hear your story."

# 8

## *Anamika*

### Few Years Ago

"Happy birthday, Anamika," Vishal uncle wished me as I offered him a piece of my birthday cake.

"Thank you, uncle," I replied.

"Hey Anamika, don't you think you are old enough to call me by my first name? After all, you are now an adult. I mean, look at you. You are now sixteen years old! I am only a few years older to you," Vishal uncle said, looking at me.

I was dressed in a pink and white salwar kameez that I had picked for my sixteenth birthday. I had left my hair open. The outfit suited my fair complexion and my light-green eyes. Everyone who saw me told me that I was looking beautiful.

"Look at me! Do I look like an uncle to you?" Vishal uncle asked, winking at me.

Vishal uncle was my father's younger brother who was in his early thirties. We lived in the same city, but he preferred to stay alone, in his own flat. He enjoyed his freedom as he travelled to different countries for work frequently.

"Then, what should I call you?" I asked innocently.

"Only Vishal. You have grown up into a beautiful girl and I am yet to marry. If a good-looking girl overhears you calling me uncle in public, do you think she will marry me?" Vishal uncle said and laughed.

"Ha ha! Okay! So from today onwards, I will call you only Vishal. Cool?" I asked.

"Yes!" Vishal said as he hugged me.

From that day onwards, Vishal uncle was no longer just my uncle; he was now more like a friend to me. We would spend a lot of time talking whenever he visited. He also became a mentor to guide me about my career options. He insisted that I concentrate on my studies. He was more like a second parent to me, who was not strict like them.

I was soon going to finish school and couldn't wait to join college. Oh, how I craved the freedom! At the same time, I had my priorities clear. I was prepared to study hard and focus on further studies.

Things were going pretty cool until that fateful night. During the middle of my final examination in the XII standard, my parents had to leave the city for three days for an emergency.

As I was in the last leg of my final exams, I needed to stay back. There wasn't any option left for me. My parents asked me if I would be more comfortable staying over at a friend's place or with Vishal. Considering that I would need my own space to study, I thought it would be best if I stay at Vishal uncle's place.

Vishal uncle would ensure that I went to sleep on time and woke up early in the morning to revise before the exam. Once I returned home from the exam, he would keep coming to my room to check on me. He would offer me snacks to ensure that I did not stay hungry and could focus better. I couldn't have been more grateful for all the support and encouragement that I received from him.

Finally, the exams were over and we decided to celebrate after the last exam. Vishal uncle ordered food from one of the posh restaurants nearby. We decided to eat at home so that we could be more relaxed. My parents were supposed to return the next afternoon.

"The dinner was awesome," I said, arranging the dinner plates in the kitchen.

"Thanks, Anamika. I ordered the food especially for you," Vishal uncle replied.

"Hmm, but after eating so much, how will I sleep?" I said, yawning.

Vishal laughed. "Go and sleep now. You have earned it after all the hard work you have put in. You are allowed to break your routine, Anamika. For a change, sleep early today," Vishal uncle suggested.

"That sounds like a brilliant idea," I agreed instantly. After all, it'd been many months that I had been compromising on my sleep to study.

I entered my room, changed into my nightdress and fell on the bed. I could barely keep my eyes open anymore now. Vishal came to the room to keep a glass of water for me.

"Good night, Vishal."

"Good night, beta. If you need anything, let me know," Vishal replied and turned the lights off before leaving.

"Please god, let me pass with good marks so that I get admission in a top college and my parents feel proud of me." I prayed as I drifted off to sleep.

♡

The next morning, I woke up groggy. My head felt heavy and lethargic.

"Oh, my head," I murmured as I pressed my hand to my forehead.

I opened my eyes slowly and noticed that my hair was no longer tied back. My chest also hurt as there were a few bruises on my upper body. I forgot the pain for a while and realized that something was very wrong. I tried getting up from the bed, but my hands didn't seem to support me. I felt very weak.

I turned my head and saw my t-shirt lying on the other side of the bed. It was the same one I had worn to bed last night. Confused and shocked, I turned my head to the other side. Vishal was sleeping next to me. And that too, naked.

My mind started to piece together the situation. I was struggling to come to terms with what had happened with me the previous night. I needed to get out of there. Maybe, this was a nightmare. How could this happen to me? I was still unable to believe it.

I gathered my strength, got up from the bed, picked up my t-shirt and ran to the bathroom. As I huddled in the corner of the bathroom under the running shower, I spent almost an hour trying to come to terms with my feelings. I felt devastated.

I opened the bathroom door slowly and stepped out.

"Hey, good morning," Vishal greeted me. He looked at me like he always did. There was no expression of guilt on his face.

"How could you?" I shouted.

"What are you saying?" Vishal asked in a calm tone.

"Don't act innocent, Vishal! I know what you did last night," I shouted. "Am I not like your daughter?" I said, throwing at him the first object that came into my hand.

"Oh, so you came to know what I did last night, haan? I realized last night that you're not a kid anymore. You have grown into a beautiful young girl," Vishal said, staring at me from top to bottom.

"Shut up, you bastard!" I screamed.

"Relax, Anamika! We are friends and this kind of stuff is perfectly fine in friendship. For god's sake, stop overacting," Vishal said casually.

"You are my father's brother, my uncle! My parents and I trusted you blindly and look what you have done to me!" I broke into tears.

"Shhh! Don't cry, Anamika! What we did last night is normal," Vishal said.

"You think I am overreacting?" I said, wiping my tears. "Just wait, Vishal. I am going to tell this to my parents. Then, see what happens," I replied in complete anger.

"Of course, you can tell your parents. But before that, have a look at these beautiful photographs on my laptop that I clicked last night," he replied and turned his laptop towards me.

I started crying as I viewed picture after picture of my naked body. I froze at the spot.

"Now keep your mouth shut before I upload these photographs on the internet and let the entire world see how beautiful you are. I also have a small video clip which I recorded last night. Do you want to see?" Vishal said, pointing at his laptop.

I felt paralyzed with multiple emotions. Only my tears were rolling down from my eyes.

"This will remain a secret between us forever, till the time you keep your mouth shut," Vishal said and walked away.

I was scared. Who could I talk to? How could I tell anyone that I had been molested by my own uncle? How would they react? What if Vishal uploaded my naked pictures? What if everyone thought that I had provoked him? I felt trapped with no option but to keep quiet. I fell on my knees, completely shaken and broken from inside.

Days passed and turned into months. By now, Vishal understood that I had decided to keep quiet, so he started approaching me again. Sometimes he called me to his house and at times, he even had the audacity to come to our place. I had become a toy for him, and molestation had become a part of my life. Several times, I thought of ending my life, but somehow could not gather the courage to do so. I had become just a body without a soul.

Months turned into years and I lost trust in everyone. I was afraid to make new friends. In college, I remained aloof from everyone. I used to lose myself in my books all the time. My close friends started noticing this change in me.

Rashmi, my childhood friend and college mate, asked mom about it when she came home.

"I think she has become more serious and focused on her career, beta," Mom replied, passing her a cup of tea.

"No aunty! We all are focused on our careers, but that does not mean we stop living our life. Can't you see a complete change in Anamika?" Rashmi said.

"What do you mean? She seems absolutely normal to us," Mom replied.

"She tries to be alone all the time. She hardly interacts with anyone, is completely engrossed in books and does not attend any social gatherings," Rashmi continued. "Something is seriously affecting her. I haven't seen her like this before; she used to be full of life," Rashmi spoke in a concerned tone.

"Don't worry about her. She is fine, and if she has any problem, she will tell us," Mom said and ended the conversation.

The only way to get out of the mess was to go away from Vishal, which is why I worked hard to achieve my goals. The same zeal saved me from depression too. Finally, because of my excellent performance at college, I was given the scholarship to pursue further studies in the USA

My parents were overjoyed on this achievement as I was the first girl from the family who was going to the USA on a scholarship programme. I was happy too, for more reasons than one. At least now, I thought, Vishal would leave me alone.

# 9

"Congratulations, Anamika," said Vishal as he approached me at the dinner party organized by my parents.

I kept looking at him, scared and frustrated at the same time.

" I know why you are looking at me like this," he said.

"Of course you know! You are the cause of everything." I wanted to blast him, but just couldn't.

"Few more days and you will be in the US. Then, I won't get such a lovely time with you again," he said.

"Lovely? Don't you realize you have ruined the most precious years of my life?" My frustration could clearly be heard in my voice.

"I know, but I could not stop myself from falling for you, Anamika. You are so beautiful," he replied.

"I was like a daughter to you, damn it!" I said as I tried to control my volume.

"I don't care. What I do care about is to be with you one last time. You know what I mean?" Vishal spoke with lust in his eyes.

"Forget it! It's not going to happen," I replied firmly.

"Please, Anamika. Look at you! You look prettier now and I cannot let you go to the US without satiating my desire for you. So just one last time," Vishal said shamelessly.

"No means no," I raised my voice a bit. Vishal took a step back.

"Okay! I think it's time to upload those beautiful photographs and video. I can do that for you if you wish to get famous before you land in the US?" Vishal said.

Silence descended between us as I was reminded of the photographs and video which he still had on his laptop. I was left with no option but to give in to his demands. I kept looking at him in anger, but that wasn't going to help.

After the party that night, mom came into my room. I was busy sending documents to the US university and was working on my laptop.

"Anamika," she said slowly. She was standing there with moist eyes.

"What happened, mom? Is everything all right?" I asked concerned.

"Anamika, my child!" She came and hugged me tight. And then, she burst into tears.

"Mom, calm down! What happened?" I asked wiping her tears.

"I am so sorry, Anamika. I was blind for all these years and did not see that my child was going through such a tough time alone." She broke down completely.

"What? What are you talking about?"

"I heard everything Vishal said to you in the evening," she replied.

I felt as if the floor had dropped off from below my feet. All these years, I had never wanted anyone to know about it. And now, my own mother knew about it. Especially, just when everything was coming to an end. I was stunned.

"Why didn't you tell us, Anamika? When it happened for the first time?" Mom asked me, but I was quiet. "Say something, beta. Please, for god's sake."

"I tried Maa, I tried." I shouted. "Not once, but several times, but backed down because I was afraid that you may not believe me."

I looked at her and let it all out. "You and dad were so concerned about my career that you never looked at what I was going through. Both of you have always been overly protective about my life, you know? You're a girl, don't do this, don't go there! So what if I am a girl, Mom? Why can't parents be open and friendly with the girls in the family? Why is it always the son who gets to enjoy a friendly and casual bond with his father? If I had been given the same confidence, I would have informed you about that incident when it happened for the first time that night," I said, wiping my tears.

"But now, the time has gone, Mom. There's no point talking about it now. He has already killed me from inside. I am just a body without a soul now."

"Don't say that, Anamika. It's not too late. I know it's our mistake, but now I am not going to spare that evil Vishal. Being a family member, he has broken our trust and has spoiled your life," she said.

"No Mom, don't think of going to the police or dare to tell this to anyone. He has my photographs and video. He may use it anywhere." She was shocked to hear that. "I beg you. Please don't create more trouble for me now."

"Don't worry, Anamika. Now there won't be any more trouble," she said and we sat hugging each other for a long time.

# 10

## At Vishal's place

"Vishal?"

"Hmm." He turned and... "Ahh!" Before he could even realize, he was stabbed with a sharp knife forcefully.

He cried louder and fell on the floor. Blood started oozing out of his body.

"Why... you...?" Vishal wanted to speak, but the pain did not let him.

"Can you feel the pain?"

"Vishal again tried to speak, "Please, please don't." He looked scared.

"I don't know what will happen after this, but I am not going to let you spoil anyone else's life. I am just going to do what I should have done earlier."

"People like you deserve an end like this. People like you, who spoil precious lives of innocent girls just for their own pleasure, are mentally sick. You don't even realize the impact your actions have on someone's life. You deserve to die a horrible death."

Vishal saw the hands coming much faster than before, but he wasn't in a condition to move. One last time, the knife went up in the air, And soon, in a full swing and with even more force, it went into Vishal.

## A few hours later

"Hi, Mom!" I said as I picked up mom's call on my cell phone. I was at home, packing my bags for the US. I had to head out in a week's time.

"Anamika, my child," she spoke. I could feel the heaviness in her voice.

"Mom, are you ok?" I asked.

"I am sorry, Anamika," she said.

"Sorry for what, Mom?" I was worried now.

"All these years, I didn't realize that my child was dying from within," she replied.

"Please don't say that," I replied, moving towards the window with moist eyes.

"Tell me if I am wrong, Anamika! As parents, we never gave you that confidence to come and discuss things with us. We used to be so concerned about your studies that we never bothered to find out whether you wanted to share anything with us other than that," she said, sobbing.

"If we would have been friendly and approachable, this would have never happened again after that night. We have failed miserably as parents," she said.

Before I could respond, she continued again, "Evil people like him are everywhere. Sometimes in the form a friend, sometimes as a neighbour, sometimes even a member from one's own family. By trusting them unquestionably, we fail to protect our own children."

"No, Mom. You and dad have been great parents. It was my mistake that I did not share this with you both. I was scared, Mom. It is not your fault," I said, trying to console her.

"Don't worry, my child. You don't have to be scared of anyone now," she said, controlling her voice.

"What do you mean?" I asked.

"No more last time, Anamika." She finally spoke.

"What? Mom, what are you saying?" I was getting tensed now.

But, she did not say a word and that scared me even more. "Please tell me, Mom. What you have done?" I shouted.

"I killed the evil that killed my daughter from within," she replied.

"What?" My heart almost stopped.

"Yes, I killed Vishal. No more last time. No more last time, my child," she said and hung up.

# 11

## Darjeeling highway

I was almost trembling. I could not believe that the innocent girl sitting in front of me had gone through so much pain in her life for years!

"Anamika," I said slowly. I noticed she had wet eyes.

"I am okay, Kabir. Don't show me any kind of sympathy," she said.

"No, Anamika. I am not showing any sympathy towards you. But..."

"But what, Kabir? I told you not to ask anything after this."

"But, aunty?"

"She is fine."

"Luckily, Vishal did not die. Mom managed to leave his place safely with the laptop and destroyed it completely. Vishal had managed to call for an ambulance, He was saved by the doctors. He was extremely scared, so he did not mention mom's name during the police complaint."

"Oh! And did you go to the US after that?" I asked.

"Kabir, you had promised that you will not ask me further questions."

"Please, Anamika. I want to know." I literally requested as I needed to know what happened after that.

"I did go to the US after that incident and obtained my Master's degree. I had started pursuing my dreams there."

"Great! Then?" I felt happy. Finally, this was turning into a story with a happy ending.

She was silent.

"Anamika I am asking you something."

"I think it's time to go, Kabir. See, the traffic has started to move," she said, pointing towards the highway.

"No, wait! I want to know more."

"No, Kabir! You have already forgotten the condition. I have told you everything I could so, let's not discuss it further," she said, picking up her bag. Her taxi, which was stuck in the traffic, had arrived now.

"Hey, wait! At least tell me where you are heading to?" I asked, trying to stop her.

"In search of a place where I can connect with myself and breathe in life again," she said and started walking towards the taxi.

"Goodbye, Kabir," she looked back and said.

"Bye, Anamika! Hope to meet you again someday," I said.

"I hope we don't meet ever again. Goodbye, Kabir," she said and got into the car.

Is this the end of our story or the beginning? I looked up and sighed.

# 12

## One year later

### December, Mumbai

I came back from Darjeeling that day, but left a part of me in that café, looking at Anamika going away. I tried searching for her through all the possible social media channels – Facebook, Twitter, Google, but could not find her. I was losing my patience because I wanted to meet her again. I don't know why, but I felt some connection with her that night. I wanted to know more about her. I wanted to know what happened once she went to the US. I was attracted to the stranger I met that night.

Day by day, I got more restless as I wanted to meet her. But unfortunately, I had no other information about that mysterious girl except her name, rather her first name only.

I even told Shruti about her. She was aware of how desperately I was looking for her. Not once had Anamika mentioned the name of the place she belonged to, or the college she had studied from, or any other thing about her that could help me find her.

Each effort made by me came to naught. I wanted to lose myself in work so that I didn't think about her anymore. But again, it was a failed attempt!

As soon as I returned to my cabin after finishing a meeting with the team members, I opened my laptop, logged in to Facebook and typed Anamika. It had become a routine for me to look for Anamika every day. I somehow felt that the best way to find her was through the internet.

I clicked on the search button and within the next few seconds, I had a huge list of profiles in front of me. It seemed never-ending. I carefully looked at the pictures of a few profiles, but as usual, it was a complete waste of time. Out of frustration, I closed the laptop screen and found Shruti standing in my cabin, staring at me.

"Done with today's search?" she asked. I didn't reply, but tried avoiding eye contact with her.

"It's been a year now, and you are still searching for her?" She asked, pulled a chair next to mine and continued. "Don't you think it's high time, Kabir? Stop thinking about her. And please, for god's sake, stop looking for her like this on the internet every single day." She pointed at my laptop. This time, I got up from my chair and walked towards the glass window.

"Look, Kabir, I know you have tried your level best to find her, but—"

"But what, Shruti? Do you have any idea how many sleepless nights I have spent looking for her and thinking about her?"

"And still, you didn't find her, right?" Shruti asked.

"No, nowhere, Shruti! Seems like I am not going to find her ever."

"Then, forget about her," Shruti said.

"Even I want to forget her, Shruti. But there is something which is pulling me towards her. I don't even know what it is." I let out a deep sigh. "At times, I feel she is somewhere very close to me but my eyes are unable to see her."

"It's all in your mind, Kabir. Stop thinking about her and life will be good again," Shruti said, keeping her hand on my shoulder.

"And for now, please concentrate on your work. We have many projects coming up," Shruti concluded. I didn't respond, just kept looking outside.

"By the way, our team is going out for dinner tonight. I hope you are coming," she said, trying to change the topic.

I turned towards her and looking at my expressions, she understood that it was a clear no from my end.

"Not again, Kabir. It's the last team dinner of the year. You can't miss this one."

"You guys carry on. I am not in the mood for any parties," I said, picking up my car keys from the table.

"Hey, wait, Kabir!" Before Shruti could stop me, I was already out of my cabin, heading home.

The year was coming to an end. People were waiting to celebrate New Year's Eve in a day. New year, new beginnings! But for me, it was of no use. After all, what was going to change in my life?

Before heading home, I decided to take a walk to get some fresh air. I wanted to get Anamika's thoughts out of my mind, at least for a while. I parked the car, pulled my tie down, kept the mobile in the car and started walking on the sea-facing promenade in Bandra. There was a high tide and the waves were hitting the rocks slowly.

I saw a few couples walking hand in hand, some kids dancing and enjoying, and also some senior citizens teaching some kids. So many diverse experiences, I thought. Many people found their destinies in Mumbai. I was yet to figure out what was written in mine.

By now, I had reached the other end of the Carter promenade and decided to have a cup of coffee at my regular café on the other side of the road. Since it was a weekday, the café was not so crowded. I was a regular visitor so the staff knew me. I sat at the table near the glass window and looked at the people sitting around me. Some were in a small group, the others were just couples who must have finished their office and were here to spend quality time with each other.

"Sir, your coffee." In no time, the waitress came and placed my coffee on the table.

"Thanks."

I was thinking about Anamika again. I jerked my head to clear away her thoughts and turned to look towards a corner. It was empty, except for one small table which was occupied by a girl sitting alone. She was busy reading a book which covered her face. I could only see her fingers.

It reminded me of Anamika. When I met her that night, she was also reading a book, just like this. I wondered if I would meet her again someday.

Suddenly, I could feel a tear rolling down from my eyes. But for whom? Just for a girl whom I had met on a highway just for a few hours? This was something very unusual.

I wasn't able to control my tears, so I moved out of the café. I kept the money on the table and gestured at the girl who had served me.

Just as I walked towards the door of the café, I saw the reflection of that girl who was reading the book. She had kept the book aside and was holding the coffee now.

Anamika! It can't be, right? It felt like an illusion. I felt dizzy and closed my eyes, just to get rid of the illusion. I opened my eyes and again I could see her reflection. My heart beat faster. She was talking to the waitress and I had no doubt it was her.

With a sense of excitement, I turned around and there she was. Anamika! God, I couldn't believe I was seeing her again.

I was already walking towards her table with a sense of excitement. "Hi Anamika," I said.

She looked up and thought for a while, looking at me. "Kabir?"

"Yes, it's me. Kabir."

"Wow, we are meeting again! I cannot believe this. But how come you are here?" She fired a round of questions.

"Should I answer standing like this or do you mind if I join you?" I said, pointing towards the empty chair next to her.

"Oh I am sorry, please have a seat," she said, keeping the book aside. "I still can't believe that we are meeting again," she said. "So, tell me how come you are here?"

"I should be the one asking you this. I had told you that I live in Mumbai," I replied.

"Oh yes! You had told me that night. I forgot," she replied sweetly.

"But I did not forget even a single thing from that night, Anamika," I said.

"Is it? But there wasn't anything as such to remember," she replied looking at me.

"That's what you think, but since the time I have returned from there, not even a single night has passed when I did not think about you," I replied.

"And what made you think about me so much?" she asked, this time looking straight into my eyes.

I did not respond. I just kept looking into her eyes. In that moment, we both just kept looking at each other.

"So, what are you doing here in Mumbai?" I asked to break the silence.

"Nothing! Just came to see Mumbai. Had heard a lot about this magical place, hence it was on my wish list. I am here to see things and to breathe in," she replied.

"Breathe in." I remembered what she meant.

"Still searching for a place to connect with yourself?" I asked.

"Yes, and seems like that search will never get over," she replied.

There was silence again. I didn't know what to say.

"So, how has life been after that night?" I asked.

"It has been the same. Why? Was it not the same for you?" she asked.

"No, not at all! I told you that I have been thinking about you and your story all the time," I said sincerely.

"And what have you been thinking about?" she asked in a surprised tone.

"Too many questions," I replied. She didn't say anything, but smiled back.

"So, what's your plan? How long are you planning to be here in Mumbai?" I asked.

"Till the time I don't get bored with this place," she replied.

"This means you are going to spend a good amount of time in Mumbai."

"It is not about the place, Kabir; it's about the people," she replied.

"I got it! I am sure you will love Mumbai."

"I hope so."

Our eyes met and this time for a longer time.

"Listen, Kabir. I have to go," she said, looking at her watch.

"Let us have dinner together and then, I will drop you wherever you want to go."

"Not possible. I am meeting someone over dinner. Maybe next time," she said.

"No way! I cannot let you go like this." I insisted.

"Kabir, next time. Please," she said and got up to leave. By the time I could have stopped her, she was already out of the café, trying to stop a taxi. I ran behind her.

"At least let me drop you wherever you want to go," I said.

"No, Kabir! I will go myself," she insisted as one taxi finally stopped and Anamika hurriedly hopped in.

I was losing out. Whatever requests I had made, she denied. "If not today, but can we spend some time tomorrow?" I requested her through the window.

"Why, Kabir? Why do you want to spend time with someone you hardly know?" she snapped.

"I thought I will take you around Mumbai and help you breathe in, and see if I can also learn to breathe in like you," I replied. "And probably, I will get to know you a little better." I finished, hoping for a positive reply from her.

She did not say a word, but smiled at me. I kept my fingers crossed for a yes.

"11' o clock, same place," she said, rushing to her handbag.

"Can I have your number, please?" I asked, looking for my cell phone. But, I realized that I had left it in the car.

"Kabir, don't worry! I will come tomorrow," she assured me.

"Promise?" I asked desperately.

"Promise, Kabir," she said and waved goodbye.

# 13

I was thinking about Anamika the entire night again, but this time, with a smile. The girl who had driven me crazy for a year was finally here. I was really excited to meet her again. The more I spoke to her, the more I wanted to know her.

Till last evening, I had no enthusiasm about celebrating the last day of the year and welcoming the new year. But today, I had a beautiful reason to look forward to the next morning.

Once up and about, I was so restless at home that I decided to head out early. I reached the cafe and waited for her. A part of me was still doubting whether she would come. It was already 11:20 and I was worried.

"Don't worry, she will come," I tried to convince myself.

And then, after a few minutes, there she was! She looked even more beautiful than before.

In her blue denim shorts, a white top and just about an inch of heels, she was looking absolutely stunning. She had put on light make up too, I noticed.

"Wow, you look beautiful!" I complimented.

"Thanks," she beamed.

"Shall we start your Mumbai *darshan*, ma'am?" I asked, bowing down chivalrously for effect.

"Yes, sir. I am all set," she replied, getting excited.

"Let's go then! Your chauffeur and the car are ready," I said pointing at my red BMW.

"Wow, I am impressed," she said, looking at the car.

"All on the company's account, ma'am."

She had a hearty laugh at that.

"So, where are we going first?" she asked, putting the seat belt on.

"I have planned the entire day and I can't be answering your questions while I drive. So just sit back and enjoy," I said.

"Ok sir, as you say."

I started driving and soon, we were out of Bandra. Talking about life and other stuff, we reached the Gateway of India.

"Wow, it's so beautiful," she said, standing in front of the impressive monument, looking at the structure and the magnificent sea-view behind it.

"Yes, it is! You should come here when it rains and when there's high tide. The waves come till here," I said, pointing at the steps.

"Must be scary also?"

"No, no! People come from all over the country to enjoy this during the rainy season." I looked at her and observed, "By the way, I hope you are not scared of water."

"Not really. Why? Are you planning to push me into the sea?"

"I won't do that, but I have some other plans," I said, amidst my laughs.

"What plans?" she asked getting curious.

"Look there!" I said, pointing at a small speed boat parked at the end of the Gateway jetty.

"Wow! Am I getting a ride in this?" She sounded exuberant, like a child.

"It's exclusively at your service, ma'am. A private speed boat just for us," I replied.

"Really?"

"Yes, Anamika," I said, looking into her eyes.

She really enjoyed what seemed like the first speed boat ride of her life. Whenever there used to be a big wave hitting the boat, she would get scared and hold my hand unknowingly.

"Scared?" I asked.

"Hmm, a bit," she replied, getting a bit conscious.

"Don't worry! I am here to take care," I replied.

She did not say a word, but went and sat on the other side of the boat.

After a nice and long speed boat ride, we again returned to the jetty.

"Kabir, can we please have something to eat. I am dying of hunger." She made a face as soon as we reached the jetty.

"Of course, we can, ma'am! A table for us has already been booked," I replied.

"Stop calling me ma'am! Don't you know my name?"

"Okay Anamika. Happy?" I said.

"Happy. But where have you made the booking?" she asked.

I twirled her around, holding her by her shoulders and said, pointing at the famous five-star hotel, The Taj Mahal Palace, Mumbai. "There!"

"Wow, it's beautiful. I have seen this only in the movies."

"So, why wait? Let's go!"

"No, I don't want to go there," she replied, looking at me.

"Why? Aren't you hungry?"

"I am, but not in the mood for the typical five-star food."

"Then, what do you want to have?" I asked.

"There is a place right behind the Taj. They make awesome kebabs," she replied.

"What? Kebabs? And how do *you* know about that place?" I was amazed.

"Heard on a vlog a few days back," she replied.

I looked at her, giving her a surprised look.

"What? Why are you staring at me? Let's go, I am starving," she said.

"You are really very mysterious, Anamika."

"I know. Now, let's go," she said and pulled my hand.

We reached the place and ordered almost all types of kebabs. We were really hungry. As soon as the order was served, we hogged everything without even talking to each other.

I looked at her, enjoying the food like a child. She was eating with her hands and her mouth was filled with food. She looked very cute. I was feeling happy just looking at her.

"The food was yumm," she said, looking at the empty plates.

"It was! Thanks for the suggestion," I replied

"Thanks, Kabir," she said.

"For this?" I asked, looking at the empty plates.

"For everything," she replied.

"Too early to say thanks; you can thank me in the evening. We still have to go and visit a few more places."

"I am so full. I don't feel like going anywhere else now," she said.

"But we still have a few good places to see," I replied.

"Hmm, can we go to just one place of my choice?" she asked.

"Of course! Tell me which place?"

"I want to go to Siddhivinayak Mandir."

"Let's go!" I said.

"But, we have a problem, Kabir."

"What happened?"

"This?" she said, pointing at her shorts.

"What? Sexy legs?" I said, without realizing what I was saying.

"Kabir!"

"Sorry." I thought for a while and said, "Hmm! I have a solution to this. Come with me!"

I took her to the Colaba street market which was just at a walking distance.

"Here, wrap this up?" I said, giving her a wrap around full-length colourful skirt.

"Not bad, Mr Kabir! I like the way you think. Quite creative!" she said.

"Thank you. Like it?" I asked.

"It's beautiful," she said.

"Then, let's go to the temple now," I said, paying for the skirt.

We reached Siddhivinayak temple and took blessings of lord Ganesha, followed by the *aarti*.

With the *pujaris* performing the aarti, the entire atmosphere turned so positive and peaceful that it felt as if all the negativity of life had ended. The mind felt free from the burden of various thoughts and the heart was filled with a new energy.

My eyes were also set on Anamika. She was enjoying the moment and looked completely lost. I could understand what 'breathe in' meant; it was truly magical. I kept looking at her and then I looked at lord Ganesha with my hands folded.

"Whatever she is praying for, please give her that. She has already gone through a lot and now deserves a good life. Please, lord, please help her." I prayed for her and soon the aarti finished.

"I really want to thank you from the bottom of my heart for this, Kabir. I wanted to visit Siddhivinayak since years and today, because of you, I was finally able to seek his blessings," she said as we walked out of the temple.

"For this, I will accept your thanks," I replied, passing her the laddu which was given as *prasad*.

"It was so peaceful and charismatic; the entire atmosphere was just mesmerizing. I could feel connected with myself, Kabir," she said while getting into the car.

"I am glad you were able to feel that. Having said that, we are not done yet."

"Oh! So where are we heading next?" She folded the skirt and put it next to her bag on the back seat. She was now back in her shorts.

"That is a surprise," I replied.

"Ok, as you say," she said, looking at the tall Mumbai buildings.

# 14

An hour later, we returned to Bandra. But this time, not to the coffee shop, but to my apartment. On the way, we saw that people had already started gathering to welcome the new year. I purposely avoided going to a restaurant or a pub. I knew that all those places would be full which is why I won't be able to talk with Anamika peacefully.

"Where have we come?" she asked as the car entered the parking lot of my building.

"That's where I live," I said pointing at a balcony.

"But Kabir, how can I—?"

"I would be really happy if you come upstairs. I will drop you back to wherever you want to go after dinner, I promise."

"But Kabir, I don't want to bother you more than I already have."

"Come on, Anamika. Consider this as my fee for taking you out for Mumbai darshan as a guide." I laughed.

"Which floor?" she asked as we entered the lift.

"Seventeenth," I replied, pressing the button. As we reached the apartment, Anamika looked around the house. She seemed pretty impressed.

"Nice apartment, Kabir," she said getting comfortable on the couch next to the small balcony.

"Thanks, but I do not own this house. This is given to me by Mr Taneja, my boss, remember? I told you," I said, passing her a glass of water.

"Oh yes, I remember."

"So, you stay alone here?"

"Absolutely alone. Why?" I asked.

"No, I thought you must be in a relationship with someone and, you know, nowadays people prefer live-in relationships," she said.

I could not control my laughter upon hearing this.

"Why are you laughing?" she asked, suddenly taken aback.

"Look at me! Do you think someone will move in with me?" I replied.

"Why, what's wrong with you? You are a young Pahadi man with an amazing job, good money and a good lifestyle. I am sure girls must be looking for a guy like you and would be desperate to move in with you."

"True, but I am not someone who believes in any short-term relationship," I clarified. "Wine?" I asked.

"Sure," she said.

I poured red wine into two glasses and prepared a cheese platter with some berries as garnishing.

"Here you go, Ms Anamika!" I said, presenting wine and an exotic food platter.

"Wow, I am impressed."

"Thanks. Cheers!"

"Cheers, Kabir!"

"So, what were you saying about a relationship?" she asked, stirring the wine slowly.

"Yes, I was saying that I believe in having a stable relationship rather than having several short-term relationships," I said.

"And why so?"

"Because for me, a relationship means being there for each other and supporting each other at all times, whether good or bad. I will go till the end with the person I love and not leave her halfway," I explained.

"I am glad to know that we still have guys like you around, who believe in long-lasting committment."

"What is your definition of a relationship?" I asked, adjusting myself on a lazy bean bag.

"I don't believe in relationships. For me, there is nothing called love," she replied.

"Oh, is it because of the tough time you had gone through?" I asked.

"Let's not talk about it," she said, finishing her drink.

"Why not?"

"Because I don't want to. I had said the last time also that we will not discuss it ever again."

"Please Anamika, why don't you let that go and start afresh?"

"How can I ever forget that, Kabir?" she replied, pouring another drink in her glass. "That bastard has ruined my life; you don't know how I was before."

She turned and looked at me. "I too had big dreams in life. I was full of hope, always ready to welcome life with arms wide open. I believed in living each moment to the fullest. But that bastard ruined everything. He killed that vibrant and optimistic Anamika. You don't know what all I have gone through, Kabir," she said.

"So, tell me, Anamika! I am here to listen to everything. Tell me what happened after you left for the US?"

She was quiet.

"Open up, Anamika. Please."

She got up from the couch. Then, she came and sat next to me on the floor, taking the support of the wall. I passed her a cushion to support her back.

"Tell me, Anamika," I said, keeping my hand on hers.

She looked at me And started off with her story. "So, I went to the US thinking that now, there would be no more trouble. And there was no trouble as far as Vishal was concerned. But the problem was here," she said, pointing at her head.

"I wanted to divert my mind and pay complete attention to my studies and concentrate on my career, but the scars of the past were deeper in my mind than I had thought."

"Oh! What makes you say that?" I asked.

"I used to keep thinking about the past. Those painful thoughts never left me alone. I tried making new friends in the US, but could not feel comfortable with them. I used to get nightmares, Kabir. I felt unsafe and insecure everywhere. Every night was scary," she continued talking and sipping her drink

"I wanted to live my life like before. I wanted to enjoy life like before. I wanted to laugh my heart out and scream to the world about my happiness. But, the thoughts of that devil did not leave my mind even for a little while."

"Hmm, any relationship back in the US?" I asked, pouring wine in my glass.

"I wanted to, Kabir. What do you think? I don't have feelings? I don't have a heart?"

"Then, what stopped you, Anamika?"

"I couldn't trust anyone, Kabir. I always feared their reaction if they got to know about my past. What if they also break my trust?" She looked at me in the eyes and completed, "What if I go through a devastating heartbreak once again?"

She looked back at her glass now. "I was going through a disappointing life anyway and did not want to make it worse. So I kept myself aloof and did not allow anyone to come close to me," she said, finishing her drink.

"Then, what happened?" I prodded her on.

"I finished my studies and started working there, but couldn't concentrate much. So, I finally decided to consult a therapist to overcome that difficult situation. I was just living for the sake of living. I was worried that if the situation still remained the same, I may get into depression and would harm myself or probably end my life."

"Oh, so what did the therapist say?"

"I was advised to move back to India to live with my family and friends so that I don't break down," she said.

"Hmm, and that's why you came back."

"Yes, I came back from the US last year and after that, with the support of my parents and friends, I slowly healed. I am not over it completely, though. So I started visiting monasteries and other peaceful places to experience serenity and peace of mind. I started reading a lot of books. I kept moving from one place to another in search of myself." she said, holding the bottle of wine in her hand now.

I guess she was drunk by then. So was I.

"Anamika, hold on!" I said, seeing that she wanted to have more wine.

"Don't stop me, Kabir. You are no one to interfere in my life," she said, drinking wine directly from the bottle now.

I didn't stop her and kept looking at her.

"Here, drink!" she said, passing me the bottle after taking a big sip.

"I am sorry I shouldn't be forcing you to say things which you don't want to share. I am just a stranger," I said.

"No! I am sorry, Kabir, I did not mean to hurt you," she said, coming close to me.

"No, but seriously Anamika, I am just a stranger to you," I said, sipping more wine.

"Yes, you were, Kabir. But not anymore." She smiled and continued, "I have enjoyed someone's company so much after years. I have laughed so much. And most importantly, at least for these few hours that I spent with you, I felt connected with my soul," she said.

"I am glad I made you happy," I said, keeping my hand on her hand.

Our eyes met and we looked at each other. Our worlds felt complete with each other.

For the next few minutes, we both were looking at each other. For a second, I felt as if my heart was urging me to hold her hand and take away all her pain. It felt as if her eyes were agreeing to my heart's desire. In the next moment, I slowly pulled her towards me. She did not react.

I caressed her smooth cheek with my finger.

"Kabir, what are you doing?" she asked softly, looking into my eyes.

"Shh! Don't say anything Anamika. I have never felt so happy in my life. I enjoyed the time spent with you so much," I said, looking at her. "Not only that time, but even right now, each minute that I am spending with you is really precious to me," I said.

"I think, I should—" she said, trying to pull her hand back from mine.

"That you should leave now, right?" I completed her sentence. "That's what you have been doing all these years, Anamika. Leaving one place and going to another. Don't run away from your life like this. Please understand that it's your life and no one else can control it. You have to face your emotions and take charge of your life. Start living it again," I said, holding her hand tighter.

She tried to look away from me.

"Look at me, Anamika! Whatever has happened is in the past now. Now, listen to your heart. Don't build a wall around it. Let the inner voice of your heart reach your mind." I pulled her closer.

"Kabir, please," she said, but did not make any effort to get away from me.

"Let it flow, Anamika. The emotions you have suppressed in your heart. Let them flow today. Do not stop them. That's when you will find yourself."

She had now closed her eyes and was listening intently to whatever I was saying.

"Look at you! How beautiful you are," I said, caressing her eyes, then her cheeks, her lips and her neck. "You are a beautiful person, Anamika and I have been dying to tell you this for so long." I kissed her softly on her shoulder.

"Kabir," she moaned.

"Let the innocent, beautiful Anamika come out. Let her live. Trust me, you will feel much better. All you need is unconditional love. And I promise to give you that."

She leaned forward and in the next moment, I felt the warmth of her lips on mine. We were kissing and it became more intense and passionate with each passing second.

My hands started to explore the beautiful curves of her body from over her clothes and she deepened the kiss. I moved forward and put my hands inside her top to feel her warm skin. We lay down on the floor, kissing each other passionately, my hands now rolling down to her shorts. I slid my hand inside her shorts to unbutton it and soon managed to do so.

She still kept her eyes closed but I knew she wanted this. The most beautiful stranger of my life was in front of my eyes.

"Anamika," I said slowly.

"Hmm?" Her voice hitched.

"I want you to look into my eyes, please."

She opened her eyes, and this time, I could sense a feeling of happiness in her. She smiled and opened up to me again. We could not stop the passion we both felt. We made love and welcomed the new year.

Indeed, this was going to be the most amazing year of my life. I was still not aware of the storm that was waiting for me next morning.

# 15

"Happy new year and a very good morning, Anamika," I said, without opening my eyes.

I did not get any response and guessed she must be sleeping. I turned towards the other side and opened my eyes, hoping to see her face first thing in the morning.

She wasn't there!

She must be in the washroom. I thought as I could not see her clothes around.

I wore a t-shirt and pyjama hurriedly and called out towards the bathroom. No response.

I knocked on the door and opened it, a couple of seconds later. She was not there.

I came to the drawing room and checked in the kitchen. "Anamika!" My heart started beating faster.

She was nowhere. I checked everywhere in the house, but couldn't find her. I opened the main door and took the lift to reach the porch.

"Security, security," I shouted.

"Ji saheb." The guard came running towards me.

"Have you seen a girl walking out of the building today morning?"

He thought for a while. "Haan, saheb. Early morning, a madam came down and asked me to stop a taxi," he replied

"Was she wearing shorts and a white top?" I asked to reconfirm.

"Ji saheb."

"Then?"

"Nothing, saheb. I stopped a taxi, she sat and left."

"Did she tell you where she wanted to go?"

"Nahi saheb. I asked her, but she did not say anything."

"But saheb—"

"But what?"

"When she sat in the taxi, I could see that she had tears in her eyes and was looking very upset."

"No, not again, Anamika. Not again," I screamed and fell on my knees.

She was gone from my life. I had lost her again.

The guard could not understand what was happening and kept looking at me.

It'd been a while but I was still on my knees, unable to accept the truth that Anamika had left me in this condition. I couldn't accept the fact that she had gone. Finally, the guard helped me to get to my apartment.

I sat on the couch next to the window. I looked towards the open sky and started thinking about Anamika. Was this a dream? Or was yesterday a figment of my imagination? Either way, I had lost her. I don't know why, but in just a few conversations, I had fallen in love with her.

As I looked at the empty wine bottle and the glass from which she drank her wine, the memories of last evening came rushing through my mind. This time, I could feel the pain even more.

As I was lost in Anamika's thoughts, I did not realize that it was almost afternoon and I had not moved an inch, until my cell phone rang.

I rushed to look for my cell phone, thinking it must be Anamika. It was Shruti.

I did not respond to her call. She called again and again and again.

Annoyed, I picked up the call when it rang for the fifth time in a row.

"Where the hell are you, Kabir?" Shruti shouted.

"I am at home," I replied.

"Home? But you were supposed to attend today's meeting! The clients are waiting," she said.

"Screw them!" I shouted.

"What! Is everything okay?" She sounded concerned this time.

I did not respond and hung up. I put the phone on the side table and an envelope caught my attention.

My name was written on the envelope and at the bottom was scribbled – Anamika.

I opened the envelope immediately and saw a letter.

*Dear Kabir,*

*When we first met that night on the highway, I didn't know we would meet like this and will come this far. We met and we spent quality time sharing our stories. I didn't know that one day, we will have another story, a story of us.*

*Maybe, it was written in our destiny to meet again. Maybe, god wanted to see me happy again which is why he sent you in my life. Yesterday, I had an amazing time after years and that is because of you, Kabir. I don't even remember the last time I had so much fun in life. You made me relive my life.*

*The last evening at your place was the most special time of my life so far. The wine, the food, our conversations, and most importantly, you – everything was special. You helped me get rid of all the negative feelings I had been carrying for years. All that hatred I used to carry in my heart had simply vanished after spending time with you last evening.*

*And finally, the way we both became one last night. It felt as if we had known each other for years. I could feel connected with you and myself. With your touch, I started to love myself again. I enjoyed each and every moment spent with you.*

*But Kabir, love and sympathy are two different emotions, and I don't want your sympathy. Yes, sympathy, Kabir. After knowing everything about me, no one will be foolish enough to love me. It may look like love at the first instance, but at the end of the day, because I have gone through so much in life, the other person will always end up showing sympathy, and not true love. I hope you understand what I am saying. I am strong enough to live my life alone. I do not need any sympathy from you or anyone.*

*You are a good person, Kabir. No need to waste your time looking for me. (You won't be able to find me and you know that already.) If it is written in our destiny, then we will definitely meet again. Otherwise, just think of it as one of the stories of your life and move ahead.*

*I am going back with lots of good memories, but most importantly, I am going back with myself.*
*Goodbye, take care.*

*Yours,*
*Mysterious girl – Anamika*

# 16

## Three months later

People say love is the most beautiful experience, but for me, it had turned out to be the most painful. The pain of not having Anamika in my life was unbearable and the worst thing was, it was increasing with every passing moment and there was no one who could pull me out of this condition, except me.

It had been three months and I was still unable to give attention to anything in my life. My passion for work, the desire to fulfil my dreams, the ambition of having a successful career – nothing was of any use. I had realized what true happiness meant to me.

Initially, I didn't even step out of the house. I spent most of the hours, sitting next to the window with the letter Anamika had left for me. I read it as many times as possible every day, and watched the sun coming up and going down. Having no phone calls and no human interactions, I just sat inside my house like a body without a soul.

I avoided calls from everyone – right from Maa, Shruti, my clients and even Mr Taneja. I was not in a condition to concentrate on anything. My mind and heart were occupied only with Anamika's thoughts and the time we had spent together. I deeply cherished the innocent bond that we had created that night in this apartment.

So what if we had spent only a few hours together! What if we probably did not know each other completely! The brief but beautiful moments that we had spent together were more than enough to create a splendid memory. After that night, I knew that at least for me, she was the one with whom I want to spend the rest of my life. I also knew that with the power of my unconditional love, I could bring her back into my life.

I rejoined the office just to avoid overthinking about Anamika. Even that didn't help much. I avoided client calls and was completely lost during meetings. I used to leave the office to meet clients but ended up being at the Gateway of India or at the Siddhivinayak Temple on most of the days, thinking about Anamika. She was there with me, breathing in the fresh air and opening her arms to cuddle the cool breeze.

At the temple, I never prayed to find her someday. I believed that she was standing beside me, attending the evening aarti. I used to look at her and smile. While taking the prasad, I used to take two laddus, one for me and another for her, believing that she was there with me.

The waiter at the kebab place, where we had visited together, always gave me a strange look as I ordered two plates of each variety of kebab and placed them on both sides of the table. She was with me, wherever I went. I could see her with me.

After returning home late every night, I used to sit next to the table where we had our last conversation while having wine. The empty wine bottles had piled up now.

The nights turned into mornings, mornings into evenings and evening became nights, but my routine was just the same. I wasn't making any effort to find her anywhere because I knew I wouldn't be able to. I let the days pass with a hope to meet her again someday.

On one such day, when I was just about to leave from the office, Mr Taneja entered my cabin. I could make out through his body language that he was annoyed with my performance in the last three months and wanted to confront me regarding the same. This was expected.

"What's wrong with you, Kabir?" Taneja asked.

I didn't get up from my chair. Just looked at him. He understood my silence, it seemed. More than my silence, my red eyes, my dull face and my dark circles must have given him signals about my condition.

He sat on a chair next to me. "Kabir, is everything ok?"

"Hmm," I replied in a dull tone.

"Doesn't look like it. Look at your condition." He sounded concerned this time.

"Yeah, seems like this is going to last forever."

"What are you saying? You are a rock star, Kabir. Tell me what has happened? I might be able to help you."

"Nothing, sir. It's personal." I gave a straightforward reply so that he didn't ask further questions.

"Oh, I see." He got up from his chair and came next to me.

"I am sure it's personal Kabir, but don't you realize that you are missing from the office most days and avoiding calls from everyone, including the clients. I mean, is this the way to handle business?" His tone changed now.

I wanted to speak further, but he started talking again. "All the clients who used to praise you for your work initially, are now complaining about your quality of work. Is this the way I am going to run my business?" This time, he banged his hand on my desk.

Business! Here, my life had gone for a toss and the gentleman sitting next to me was only thinking about his business! I thought, staring into his eyes, but didn't say a word.

"I understand sir, but I am unable to concentrate—"

"Till when? It's been three months!" He looked straight into my eyes, expecting an answer. "Give me a time frame. I can't be waiting for your personal problems to get resolved and lose my business like this," he said, lighting up his cigar.

"I don't know, Mr Taneja. I really don't see a way out."

"Kabir, you were never like this. I have always seen a spark in you. Look at your face! This unkempt look, these dark circles under your eyes and the pale skin. That's not you, Kabir."

He was right. It had been months now and whatever Mr Taneja said was true.

"You know what? I really don't know what your problem is but I can't be losing business because of it. What I strongly feel is that either you bounce back or..." He stopped.

"Or what, sir?" I asked.

"Kabir, don't misunderstand me, but for now, I think you should take a break. You really need it." He let out a deep breath and said, "Do one thing, go somewhere and enjoy your life. Have fun. Come out of this situation and we can complete this discussion once you return."

I just looked at him. Maybe he was right. I certainly needed a break from this city. I had been running like a headless chicken to fulfil my dreams. But today, it was of no use because I had realized that true happiness was being with someone whom you love. Everything else is just a worthless part of life.

"Are you listening to me?" Mr Taneja asked.

"Yes, I am listening to you, sir," I replied.

"Good! Go home for a few days and come back like a champion," Mr Taneja advised and turned to leave. "By the way, where are you planning to go Kabir?" he asked.

"Somewhere I can connect with myself and can breathe in life once again."

# 17

**Bangkok, Thailand**

"*Sawadee ka!*" The receptionist greeted as soon as I reached at the reception to check in at the tallest and the most luxurious hotel of Bangkok – The Tower Club.

"Hi, I have a reservation. My name is Kabir Shergill."

"Sure, sir. I will help you with that in a moment. Can I please have your passport, sir?"

I handed over my passport to her. She smiled and after completing the necessary formalities, handed over the key card to my room.

"As requested, your suite is on the sixty-second floor and it also has a private terrace. We are sure you would enjoy the view of the entire Bangkok from there. It's very beautiful," the receptionist said.

"Thanks," I said, picking up my passport from the counter.

"He will bring your luggage to your suite," the receptionist said, pointing at a concierge.

"Sure, thanks."

I reached the sixty-second floor of the hotel and the concierge escorted me to my suite. It was a huge luxurious suite that I had booked. It had all the ultra modern amenities, right from a huge round bed, a luxurious Jacuzzi, to a lavish bar counter. But what grabbed my attention was the open terrace of the suite.

I opened the huge sliding door of the terrace. The view was just mind-blowing. Since it was early in the morning and the sun had slowly started to rise, the view was beautiful. With the rising sun, the fog started to uncover the beauty of this amazing city. Even the other surrounding tall buildings were looking quite small in comparison to where I was standing.

This was the second week of my break. I had earlier spent a week in a resort in a less populated area in Kerala. The resort was known for its ancient Ayurveda therapies to release stress and anxiety.

I spent each morning, taking ancient Ayurveda therapies for mind and body alignment. The rest of the day passed by taking multiple walks within the resort, taking small boat rides in the backwaters and sitting quietly on the banks. Each evening passed by watching the beautiful sunset and breathing in life.

In the last one week, I had realized the importance of spending time with our own self. I enjoyed my visit to Kerala and wanted to extend it. But despite the therapies reducing my stress level a bit, I realized that I still had a long way to go.

In order to do so, I decided to explore the never-sleeping Bangkok. Since my nights were mostly sleepless, this was a perfect destination.

I quickly freshened up as it was now time for me to explore the beauty of this city. Soon, I headed to the famous Wat Pho, which is the temple of the reclining Buddha. The receptionist suggested that since I was the only one travelling, the best way to dodge the Bangkok traffic was to take a bike taxi. I must say, she was right!

Once I reached my destination, I removed my shoes. As suggested by the bike taxi rider, I also purchased a bowl of coins which he said I should drop in the 108 bronze bowls which were placed on the walls throughout the temple. He also said that while dropping coins into those bowls, I should make a wish which would definitely come true. Since I had only one wish at that point in time, I did so with complete faith.

As I walked inside the hall, I started dropping coins in each bowl and wished that I meet Anamika soon. Since it was still early in the morning, the monks were chanting. I sat in a corner and observed them pray until they finished the morning rituals.

It felt as if Anamika was sitting right beside me. I could see her looking at me and smiling. It felt as if we were both connected, our heartbeats were in complete sync with each other.

The connection was so strong and magical that it brought a smile on my face.

It happens in love that you start seeing that person in front of you even though that person isn't there. That's the power of true love. I realized it for the first time amidst the pious chanting.

I spent almost the entire day at the temple, not wanting to return because that place had brought a smile on my face. More than that, the faith which was dying in some corner of my heart, was alive again.

It then became a routine for me to start my day by coming to this temple and breathe in life, just like Anamika would have done. I had started living her life and did everything that Anamika would have done. I spent a lot of time in the temple, watched the monks chanting, took walks in the monastery campus, smiled for no reason and felt happy.

The other half of the day was spent on exploring the other side of the city and visiting the local places. With just a small bag pack on my shoulder, no cell phone (as I wanted to disconnect from everyone), no camera (as I wanted to capture these moments in my heart and mind and not on any electronic device) and no predefined plan for the day, I just wanted to go with the flow. I visited almost every corner of the city.

It felt good because this was for the first time after joining BIM that I was living my life once again. Instead of taking a cab, I took trains, travelled in local transport and hopped on to bike taxies. I covered as many places as I could, tried various local Thai dishes at the roadside stalls and interacted with the unknown but friendly Thai locals. It was a profound sentiment which could only be felt and not expressed.

I was enjoying each moment and living life the way Anamika must be living somewhere right now, even if she was away from me!

# 18

## *Anamika*

### Around the same time, somewhere in Bangkok

Only a few hours were left for me to return to India. This seemed to be my last travel. I didn't know if I would ever travel again like this. In the previous few years, I had tried my level best to find myself. I travelled wherever possible in search of peace and to connect with myself once again. But honestly, that didn't help much.

On the other hand, the most beautiful part of my journey of finding myself happened when I met Kabir. I would always cherish the time I spent in Mumbai with Kabir. No one had made me feel special the way Kabir did. I had lost all hope of finding myself, but it was Kabir who entered into my life and added colours to it.

That one day, that one night in Mumbai with Kabir, has brought so much happiness and hope in my life and I am going to spend the rest of my life remembering that beautiful time. It has been months, but I still feel as if Kabir is around me. I don't know why, but I am just not able to let Kabir out of my mind and heart.

I wish I could go back to Kabir, but knowing everything, I don't want to spoil his life. He deserves someone better and I am sure he will move on without me, sooner or later.

Here I was, ending my trip in Bangkok, knowing that Kabir was far away in Mumbai. I didn't know why, but my heart felt as if he was somewhere here only.

Thinking about my memories with Kabir, I had reached the end of the lane and saw a dead end ahead. Guess this was a signal god wanted to give. I looked back; I had come a long way.

I looked at the other side to see many restaurants. I was tired and decided to have a cup of coffee before I headed to the airport.

I came across a restaurant with a tag line which read, Indo Pak. Because love doesn't believe in borders. The name was quite catchy so I decided to visit it. I walked inside and an elderly couple acknowledged me as I passed the billing counter.

It was a nicely decorated restaurant with love quotes written on one side of the wall and the other wall had posters of famous Hindi romantic movies and some in Urdu, probably some Pakistani movies I guessed. It was not dinner time yet so only a few customers were there. I took a corner table and glanced through the menu which was kept at the table.

"Hello ma'am," greeted the old man who was at the counter. He was tall and must be in his late fifties, however, he still had a charm on his face.

"Hello," I wished back

"Sorry, but it's not dinner time yet. I am afraid we can't make a complete dinner order," he said apologetically.

"Oh, that's perfectly alright. I am fine with a cup of coffee if that is possible."

"Definitely ma'am." He smiled and went back.

I was looking at him from the distance. I was impressed by the way he was smiling and interacting with every possible customer and the way he was instructing the staff. In between, he went back to the lady who was handling the counter and whispered something to her. And then, they both laughed. Looking at this, I was convinced that he was the owner of the restaurant.

In the next few minutes, the man along with the waiter walked towards my table. The waiter placed a cup of hot coffee and some bread rolls.

"Thanks," I said. "But I only needed coffee."

"Have it beta, these are delicious," insisted the man. The way he said it, I didn't find it appropriate to deny his request.

"Thank you, sir," I replied.

"Baktawar Khan. People here call me Khan baba," he introduced himself.

"I am Anamika,"

"Indian?" he asked.

"Yes, Khan baba. And you?"

"From the past thirty years, I am settled here. But originally, I am from Pakistan," he said, occupying the vacant chair.

"Oh, I see! By the way, the name of your restaurant is very unique. I haven't come across such a name anywhere," I said, sipping the coffee.

"I know, it's the name that attracts customers here." He smiled. "Having said that, the food that we serve here is one of the best in Bangkok," he said and laughed.

"So what's the story behind the name?"

"That's a long story, my child."

"I am sure you can share it with me Khan baba. You still have time for the customers to walk in for dinner," I said and smiled at him.

"Hope you are not a journalist."

"No, I am just a just an explorer, trying to connect with myself once again," I clarified.

He looked into my eyes for a few seconds and then, he signalled a waiter to bring a cup of tea for him.

# 19

## Khan baba's story

"I am from Pakistan, and you see her, she is my wife Maithili. She is from India." He pointed at the lady at the cash counter.

"Wow, sounds like an amazing story. How did you both meet?"

"Well, back in those days, I was a journalist in Pakistan and was living in Karachi. It was thirty-two years back when a few Pakistani journalists got an invitation from the Indian government to cover an Indo-Pak conference in New Delhi."

"Hmm," I nodded.

"It was a five-day long event and we were staying in the same hotel where the conference was taking place," he said, sipping his tea. "At the hotel, I saw this beautiful young Indian girl at the reception and was mesmerized by her beauty. It was love at first sight for me."

"Great! Then?"

"Then what! If she was beautiful, I was also no less. Back then, I was young, dynamic, and a well-built Pakistani guy."

"You are still handsome, Khan Baba."

"This is nothing. Back then, it was different." He smiled.

"Then, how did you make your first move? I mean, how did you approach ma'am?"

"I desperately wanted to initiate a conversation with her. The best way was to ask questions about places to visit in Delhi and that's how we started talking. She used to reply politely with all the information. When she talked, I couldn't get my eyes off her eyes. I guess she noticed that."

"I am sure she did." I said, thrilled.

"After the conference, I used to run towards the staff exit and wait for her to take a cycle rickshaw to her place. Then, I used to follow her till the gate of her colony."

"Oh! You followed her. But, did you also talk to her? I mean, you had very limited days in India, right?"

"Yes, I did! The night I was supposed to return to Pakistan, I waited for her at the staff exit. She finished her duty and I started following her. After a while, she noticed me. In a lonely lane, she asked the rickshaw guy to stop and got down."

"Then?"

Khan Baba continued.

She came towards me and said, "It's been four days and I am noticing that you are following me. What do you want sir?"

"I am Baktawar Khan."

"Maithili Sharma," she replied.

"I know your name sir. I could see that on your passport and in the hotel reservation form."

"Oh!"

"So, tell me. Why are you following me every day?"

"Don't take me wrong Maithili, but I don't have enough time. So I will come to the point straight away."

There was no one around us; it was an empty lane next to a playground where a few kids were playing cricket. "I know that we both don't know anything about each other. And, at this point, I may sound a bit weird, but I have fallen in love with you," I opened my heart without any hesitation.

She looked at me and didn't say a word. I guess she was shocked.

"Fallen in love? In just four days? Don't you think it's too quick?"

"No, I don't think so. Because love doesn't follow any timeline. It just happens, like it has happened to me."

"It can happen in your Pakistan, but not here, Sir,"

"Stop calling me 'sir'. My name is Baktawar."

She sighed and then spoke again. "Look Baktawar, for me, you are just a guest staying at the hotel where I work. Nothing beyond that," she said and started walking. "And, it would be better if you don't follow me anymore," she concluded.

"Of course, I understand that. I don't have any right to follow you. I guess I will have to return with these memories then," I said in a dull tone.

"Memories? When did we create them?" Maithili stopped and turned towards me.

"When I saw you for the first time at the hotel reception, from that moment to this time, they are all lovely memories for me," I said and continued. "Your beautiful eyes, your humble way of connecting with everyone, the way you smell the fresh flowers kept at the front desk every morning and your innocent smile. For me, all these are precious memories that I am going to take back with me."

She blushed but did not say anything.

"Hope I am not making you uncomfortable by saying all this," I asked and walked towards her.

She started walking again and I accompanied her. She didn't mind.

"So where do you live in Pakistan?" she asked.

"I live in Karachi with my Ammi and Abbu. How about you?"

"Hmm, I live with my parents and two younger sisters. You know the address very well already." She smiled. "So, have you visited any places in Delhi or is it just from the hotel to my colony?"

"Just hotel to your colony," I replied, looking at her.

She looked at me and it felt as if she was enjoying this little conversation too.

"*Chaat*?" she asked pointing at a road-side stall making hot aloo tikki chaat.

"This?" I asked pointing at the stall.

"You are in Delhi, Mr Baktawar. People say if you don't try the special *aloo tikki* chaat, then your trip to Delhi is incomplete." She smiled and looked at me.

"Well, in that case, let's go," I said.

We reached the stall and Maithili ordered two plates of chaat which he served with lots of chhole. It looked delicious.

"How's it?" she asked as I took the first bite.

"Hmm, it's delicious Maithili."

I paid the guy and with the chaat in hand, we started walking again. We spoke about our families and cultures, our likes and dislikes, cinema and music. Truly, our culture, religion, and countries were different, but we realized that we also had a lot of similarities. For instance, we both liked cinema and our thoughts towards religion and people matched.

We had now reached near her colony. Maithili turned towards me and said. "You must leave now Baktawar." She looked around to ensure no one was looking at us.

"Don't worry. I don't want to create any troubles for you," I assured.

"Thanks for walking with me till here."

"I am leaving tonight, so it's time to say goodbye." She stared at me as I said, "Goodbye, Maithili."

"Bye, Bakatwar."

I looked at her as she entered her colony gate and kept looking until she was gone. Yes, away from my eyes, but never from my heart. That night, I left for Pakistan and left a small note for her at the reception.

*Maithili, there are some relationships that we can name, but ours is one of those that cannot be given a name. However, it's always good to know that you have a friend in a country where no one knows you except that one person. I am going back with the same feeling. Goodbye, Maithili.*

Khan baba paused for a while, and I noticed I had already finished my coffee.

"Wow. This was amazing." I told him. "But what happened after this?"

"My heart was full of her. It kept telling me that love knows no border. Love doesn't care for any religion. It's a pure and unconditional emotion after all, isn't it?" Khan baba said, keeping his hand on his heart.

"Considering the tough time India and Pakistan was going through, it was difficult to go back to India. So I wrote her the first letter, expressing how I was feeling after coming back and sent it to the hotel address."

"Wow! A love letter across the border? This is so amazing! Did she read and reply to it?"

"No, but I wasn't going to give up so easily. I kept sending her letters for the next six months, expressing my feelings for her. In every letter, I used to mention my feelings and how my world was incomplete without her. I used to ask the whereabouts of her family, write the details about my family, the projects on which I was working on, the vibrant and colourful local fairs which were going on in Karachi, our festival and the delicious Indian dishes that I was enjoying."

He smiled fondly, reminiscing, "Through my letter, even though she was in India, I wanted to make her feel as if she was right here in Pakistan. I don't know why, but whenever I wrote a letter, I felt closer to her. It happens when you love someone truly, doesn't it?" Khan baba asked, looking at me.

"I understand," I said and smiled.

"I waited for at least one reply from her side, but it never came. So one day, I decided to call her up. I went to a telephone booth and dialled the hotel's number in Delhi when she was on duty."

"Welcome to Hotel Delhi International. This is Maithili. How may I assist you?"

"As-salamu alaykum, Maithili ji."

"Baktawar!" she said, after a while from the other end. To hear my name from her was the most amazing feeling.

"Yes, it's me Baktawar. How are you Maithili?"

"Hmm, good, but why have you called?"

"To speak to you."

"But why?" she whispered.

"You know the reason very well. Do I still need to mention it?"

There was no reply from her end. I looked at the ISD rate machine. It was racing like anything, but I was enjoying this silence between us.

"Have you been reading my letters or throwing them in the bin?"

"I have been reading all of your letters, Baktawar."

"Then, why aren't you replying to it? Have I written anything which I shouldn't be writing?"

"No, nothing as such, but there is no point in replying."

"Why?"

"Because... I mean what you have written about us being together, you know that's not possible because—" she wanted to say more and I completed her sentence.

"Because I am a Pakistani and you are an Indian?"

"And because you are a Muslim and I am a Hindu," she concluded.

"But, not because you don't have feelings for me, right?"

She didn't reply.

"Please tell me if you don't have any feelings for me so that I get a definite answer and do not bother you again."

Still, there was no reply from her end.

"I have understood your silence, Maithili. I know what your heart is saying but I want to hear it from you," I said. I was desperate to hear her feelings for me, but she remained silent.

"Don't worry. I am not going to force you for anything Maithili. For me, the only happiness is knowing that you are reading my letters. That's more than enough for me."

"Baktawar, I will have to hang up now. A few guests are walking towards the reception."

"I know we are not going to talk after this, but still, there will be hope in my heart to receive a letter from you someday." I wanted to say more, but she interrupted.

"Thank you for calling Hotel Delhi International. Have a nice day," she said and disconnected the line.

"Oh, that's sad," I said, looking at my empty cup of coffee.

"Why sad? That was the happiest day because I came to know that she also had feelings for me."

"But, she never said anything!" I was surprised now.

"Her silence, beta! Her silence was much louder than the words that I was expecting. It was a heart to heart connection, you see."

We were still talking when the beautiful lady herself walked towards us.

"Don't tell me you have started narrating our story again," she said, standing next to him.

"Story! How can you call it a story?" Baktawar said to Maithili.

"Because that's what you love doing," she said and took a chair next to him.

"Hello ma'am. I am Anamika."

"Maithili. Mrs Maithili Baktawar Sharma." She turned to Khan baba and asked, "So, till where has your story reached Khan Sahab?" She took a sip of tea from his cup.

"Tilll when we spoke for the first and last time on the call."

"Yes, please tell me what happened after that call, Maithili ji?" I asked curiously.

"So back in Pakistan, he was waiting for a letter. I, on the other side, didn't write to him any. But, one day, I sent a telegram on the address mentioned in his letters."

"*A friend in a country where no one knows you, needs your help, please call*," Khan baba replied, taking out the telegram from his pocket. I looked at the telegram, overjoyed.

"And after reading the telegram, I immediately ran to make that one call."

"Thank god, you called." She was almost crying when she picked up the call.

"I had to. After all, a friend needs my help."

"What happened, Maithili? Why are you crying?"

"'Baktawar, my parents have found someone and have fixed my marriage," came the shock of my life from her end.

"Oh, so you sent a telegram to invite me to your wedding?"

"No no! I asked you to call because I... I don't want to marry someone else... because..."

"Because what, Maithili?"

"Because I want to be with someone whom I have known for all these months."

"And who is this someone?"

"You, Baktawar!"

"What?" I wasn't expecting this.

"Yes! All these months, reading your letters, I have known you as a person. I have realized your feelings for me and every word in your letter has made me fall for you, Baktawar," she said and continued. "Each day when I used to return home, it used to feel as if you are still following me. It felt as if you were there, watching me from the gate of the colony where you had left me the last time. This doesn't happen until it's love, right?"

"Who knows it better than me, Maithili! But then, why haven't you told me this earlier?"

"Because of this society, the people around us, our religions and our countries. You know how difficult it is, but now when I know that I have to spend my life with someone whom I don't even know, it's difficult. I am not going to do that," she said.

"I won't let it happen either," I assured her.

"Take me from here, Baktawar. I can't be here anymore."

"Oh Maithili! I also want to be with you."

"What do we do now Baktawar?" she asked.

I thought for a while and said, "Look Maithili, it is unlikely that you can shift here to Pakistan or I can shift to India. So let's look for a place where we don't need to lose our identities. A place where you can be what you are and I can be myself. And most importantly, where we can be together forever."

"I agree with you, Baktawar, but I don't have time. Whatever you want to do, do it fast," she said.

"I will Maithili, don't worry. Together we will create a world where love will be our identity and nothing else will matter. Very soon, we shall be together. Just have faith in me."

"I trust you Baktawar."

"'I love you Maithili."

"I... I love you. I love you too Baktawar. Just take me from here."

"Soon Maithili," I said and we hung up.

"Wow! So finally, it was time for both of you to be together." I was ecstatic.

In the next few days, I made all the arrangements for her to travel to Thailand and for myself to reach there from Pakistan. We both chose a country where no one knew us and the rest is history," Baktawar said, holding Maithili's hand.

"That's amazing!" I looked at Maithili and asked, "But ma'am, can I ask you a question?"

"I know what you going to ask Anamika, still go ahead," she replied and looked at Baktawar.

"You met him just once. He was from another country. You spoke to him just twice over calls and read his letters. Was that enough for you to take such a step that you left everything in India for him?"

"I agree with all of that, but the biggest foundation of any relationship is trust. If you don't have that, you can't succeed in this journey, Anamika," Maithili replied. "As far as love is concerned, you don't need other reasons. Love itself is enough. Anamika, if you see that true love for you in someone's eyes, nothing else is needed," Maithili said, looking at Baktawar. He kissed Maithili's hand.

"Imagine what could have happened if I would have doubted him and did not come here? We wouldn't have been together forever, right?" Maithili spoke. "But here, I am with him, living a life which I had only dreamed of. I don't have any regrets," Maithili said happily.

"We are happy together in our lovely nest," Khan baba said, pointing at the wall full of romantic quotes.

Indeed, I could see immense love in their eyes. They were truly meant for each other. For the first time in my life, I had witnessed the power of love and faith. It was incredible. I was truly mesmerized after listening to their story, forgetting the difficult situation I was in.

"So Anamika, what's your story?" Maithili asked me.

I smiled and got up from my chair.

"Where are you going, beta?"

"Wish I could answer that question, Khan baba. But honestly, I don't know where my destiny will take me. I have to go," I sighed and replied. They noticed the sadness in my eyes.

Both of them looked at me and then, looked at each other. Mrs Maithili Baktawar got up and kissed my forehead.

I reached the door, turned towards them and said, "And if it is in my destiny to find myself back, then one day I will come back and narrate my story to both of you."

I got into the cab and headed towards the airport to catch a flight to India. Sitting in the cab, thinking about Khan baba and Maithili's love story, reminded me of the time that I had spent with Kabir. About the letter I had left for him that night. I began to think if I was heading in the right direction.

I was hoping to make it to the airport on time, but the roads were choking with traffic. I had to reach India anyhow. Dr Neha had told me something I wasn't expecting and suggested that I should return to India as soon as possible. I needed immediate medical attention.

It had started drizzling so the traffic was moving a little slower than usual. The cab stopped at the crossroads as the signal had turned red now.

From inside the cab, I tried looking at both sides, but because of the raindrops on the windowpane, the visibility was very less.

I looked at my watch, sighed, and looked outside again, hoping for the signal to open.

And then, out of nowhere, I saw a bike taxi with a pillion, coming and stopping just adjacent to my cab.

There were still sixty seconds left for the signal to turn green. While everyone was eager to move ahead, there was this pillion on the bike taxi who had earphones plugged in. Deep in the middle of chaos, he was hammering his head to the beats and one could make out that he was enjoying the music. He was in no hurry at all. Rather, he was enjoying this moment and the drizzle.

I was looking at that guy when he suddenly removed his helmet. With his face looking up at the sky, he opened his arms to enjoy the rain. I couldn't believe my eyes.

Was I dreaming? No, I wasn't! I cleared the fog on the inside glass of the car window with my bare hand and looked closely at the guy.

Yes, it was Kabir! Right in front of my eyes, enjoying and living in the moment. He looked so carefree. My heart was filled with excitement and joy. I tried to lower the glass down but I just couldn't do it. The thought of what I had written in my letter to him, how I left him that morning without telling him anything, and the situation that I was now going through flashed in my mind in a fraction of seconds. I just couldn't muster the courage to face him.

He, on the other hand, wasn't bothered with who he was surrounded by. He was in his own world, with his eyes closed and face still looking at the sky. Now, only ten seconds were left for the signal to turn green.

Tears rolled down from my eyes as I wasn't able to do anything. Looking at him like this, I could make out that he was happy in his life and had moved on. I didn't want to interfere in his life and give him any more trouble.

It was time. The signal turned green and the cab started moving. I kept looking at him and then, as destiny wanted, his bike taxi took a left, while my cab took a right. It was a sign that our paths were different.

That night, I returned to India where destiny was ready to take yet another turn in my life!

# 20

## *Kabir*

Lack of sleep and the thoughts of Anamika were the two main reasons why I was sitting at The Drinker's Den, the famous pub in Bangkok. I needed a drink and this was the place.

I had been to many pubs in the past but Drinker's Den was different. It was a huge pub, having the largest bar counter I had ever seen. It served a variety of alcohol from across the world and all the variety that one could imagine. With cosy couches in the dark corners of the pub and the DJ playing the best of music, this place felt out of the world indeed.

It was a Friday night and as Bangkok is known is for its night parties, I was truly witnessing the same. People from all age groups were drinking, dancing and enjoying with their partners. Looking at their enthusiasm and wild partying, it felt as if there was no tomorrow. They only wanted to live in the present moment.

Seeing all those couples, I missed Anamika a lot. I felt a desperate need to complete our story. But I didn't know how. I kept thinking about finding her. The first drink led to the second, the third one to the fourth and then, I stopped counting.

In that dimly lit pub, I could see Anamika everywhere. With every flash of light, she was appearing, and just when I blinked my eyes, she was gone.

I wondered what a life I had! People thought I lived a great life with all luxuries. Often, they felt jealous of my success, my well-paying job, and my trips to various countries. What else could one ask for!

I had all the reasons to feel happy, but here I was! Having everything, but not her. I was nothing. All these materialistic things didn't give me happiness.

I had been drinking for a while and decided to move out. The lights and sound, along with the constant appearances of Anamika made me feel dizzy. I tried getting down from the high-rise bar chair but couldn't control myself. I was about to fall when someone extended support.

"Careful!" I heard a female's voice as her hands supported my shoulders.

I looked up at a young blonde smiling at me.

"Thanks," I said, trying to take control of my falling body.

"I hope you are ok," she said, helping me sit back on the bar chair.

"Yeah! I mean, I am kind of okay. Thank you once again."

I looked at her carefully. She was a beautiful blonde girl, wearing a flashy black jacket with a white low cut short dress which displayed enough of her well-toned figure.

"Seems like you've had enough drinks," she said, smiling at me. She sat on a chair next to mine.

"I think so," I replied, looking at her.

"Are you alone or is there someone whom I can call to accompany you, sir?"

"There is no one with me. I am all alone."

"Hmm, solo travel! I like that," she said.

"Yeah, it's kind of good," I replied, trying to control my falling face.

"By the way, my name is Kate," she said, extending her hand for a handshake.

"Kabir. I am Kabir," I said, shaking hands with her.

"Nice name," Kate replied. "From India?"

"Yes! How about you?"

"Sweden."

"Great! Are you here on a holiday, Kate?"

"It's holiday plus work," Kate replied and winked at me.

"It's a nice place for holidaying, but work? What kind of work?" I asked, sipping some water.

"Oh, I work here in this pub and my job is to ensure that I accompany people like you, who are here on a solo journey," Kate said, pointing at me. "I take care of them, spend time with them and you know, have a little fun." Kate leaned forward towards me and ran her soft figures over my neck.

"Oh, I see! I get it, ma'am."

"Now you have understood." She smiled and asked, "Drinks?"

"No, I have had enough. If I drink more, I am going to lose control and it would be difficult to reach back to my hotel."

"Oh, c'mon my friend! It's Bangkok, the most happening city, and you are here for fun. It's okay to go out of control sometimes. And don't worry about reaching back to the hotel. I am here to take care of you," Kate said and smiled.

I was already a bit high and was losing my senses. On the other hand, to be honest, I didn't want to say no to such a beautiful girl.

"What would you want to have?" I agreed to another round of drinks.

"My favourite, tequila shots!" Kate replied.

I smiled at her and looked at the bartender.

"Two tequila shots, please."

The very next minute, the bartender kept two tequila shots in front of us. "Cheers to this wonderful night," Kate said, passing me a shot.

"Cheers!"

Within seconds, I could feel the tequila going down through my throat to my stomach, giving me a light burning sensation.

"Wow! That was awesome, wasn't it?" she asked.

"I don't know if it was awesome. But, sitting here, even when I am not moving, the floor in front of my eyes is spinning and dancing," I replied.

She laughed. "It happens, my friend. This is just the beginning of the fun. I told you that my job is to ensure that you have a good time here," she said and placed her hand on mine.

The music got louder and I could see people going crazy on the beats.

"So, why solo travel?" Kate came a little closer and asked loudly as the music was too loud.

I shrugged.

"What do you mean by that?" she asked.

"I don't have any particular reason to travel solo. I just wanted to get back to my life. I wanted to spend some time alone, so that I could connect with my soul," I said.

"Wow! You look too young to be talking so philosophically," Kate said.

"Life teaches you everything. And when life gives lessons, it doesn't look at the age, it just teaches," I said and signalled at the bartender for repeat shots.

"Seems like something is bothering you," Kate asked.

"Nothing," I replied, passing her the shot.

We picked up our shots and finished it even faster this time.

"Dance?" she asked.

"No, Kate. I am really not the guy you would enjoy dancing with."

"Don't be shy! I am sure I am going to enjoy dancing with you, Kabir. And even if I don't enjoy, I will make sure you enjoy it," she said and pulled me to the dance floor.

The alcohol inside my body wasn't allowing me to move even an inch. My vision was blurry, and the dance floor itself was dancing in front of me. I was just standing and looking at Kate. Her dance moves were crazy enough to attract any guy from the dance floor and make him fall for her.

Kate saw me noticing her and came closer to me. She put my hands on her slim waist. I was standing still, but could feel her body with her each dance move. She moved close enough and now, we were facing each other. I could now smell her perfume.

This setting, the influence of alcohol and her hair falling on my face, were driving me to the next level. Surely from her side, these moves were intentional, and from my end, I was unable to do anything.

In those moments, I forgot everything. I forgot my worries, my sufferings and my reason of taking this break. I only wanted to live in that moment. I didn't know if it was the alcohol or Kate's company, but it felt good.

Kate brought some more shots in between and made me drink. I was now losing my focus. I felt like throwing up, but controlled it. I wanted to move out but I wasn't able to even walk properly. I slowly moved towards a corner to take a seat. Kate came along with me.

"Are you ok, my friend?" Kate asked.

"No, it's too much alcohol inside me now. I should return to my hotel," I managed to say.

"Ok, but how will you go?"

"I will manage," I said and tried getting up from the chair. I just couldn't.

"Do you mind if I drop you to your hotel?" Kate asked.

"No, I mean..." I wanted to say no to her, but before I could say a no, she interrupted.

"I told you in the beginning that I will take care of you. Don't worry! I am here and the night is still young. Let me accompany you till your hotel," she said, keeping her hand on my lap.

In the next few minutes, after settling the bill, we walked out of the pub. Kate was holding my hand.

"How do you want to go?" Kate asked.

"A cab maybe."

"My friend, you are in Bangkok. Then, why take a cab?"

"Then, how shall we reach? I am in no condition to walk that much."

"We don't need to walk. We can go by that," she said, pointing to a well decorated tuk-tuk, the Thai auto-rickshaw.

"Oh, that! What do you call this? Tuk-tuk, right?"

"Yes! You will enjoy this ride and it's open, so by the time we reach, you would feel much better because of the fresh air. If you feel better, we can probably have more drinks," she said and smiled.

"No please, no more drinks. My capacity is over. If I drink more, I am going to pass out."

"Well, I don't want you to pass out. I want you to be in your senses so that you experience some more beautiful time with me for the rest of the night." She winked again. "And don't worry. Until you don't feel better, I am not going to leave you. So, rest assured, you are in safe company, Kabir."

"I see that," I said and looked at her.

"Where are you staying?"

"Tower Club."

"Oh wow! That's an amazing place. What are we doing here then? Let's go!" she said and pulled me to the tuk-tuk.

We hopped right in, making our way to the hotel. The driver was passing through other vehicles at a fast pace, with Kate shouting in her excitement. Very soon, we reached the hotel. As Kate had said, it was indeed a fun ride.

# 21

We got into the lift and pressed the button for the sixty-second floor. Kate was still holding my hand and looking into my eyes, which made me a bit conscious. Soon, we reached outside my room.

I tried opening the room with the key card, but in my condition, I was unable to open it even after multiple attempts. Kate looked at me and laughed. "Wait! Let me help you with that," she said.

"Welcome," she said, escorting me carefully inside my own room.

"Thanks, Kate," I said, throwing myself on the couch.

"Thanks for what, Kabir?"

"If not for you, I wouldn't even have reached the hotel," I replied.

"I told you that's my job," Kate said, sitting next to me on the couch.

"You are a really nice girl, Kate." I said, in my drunken stupor.

"And you are a nice guy too," she said, playing with my hair.

"Go help yourself with the drinks. The bar is right there," I said, pointing to the in-room bar counter.

"Thanks! Would you like to have something?" she asked.

"Whatever you are having. I will just give you a little company."

Kate went to the bar and picked a wine bottle, two glasses and then, adjusted the room lighting to dim mode. From the distance, I saw her walking towards me and for once it felt as if Anamika was walking towards me. I looked at her carefully.

I kept looking at her until she reached me. I tried widening my eyes to look at her properly.

"What are you looking at so carefully?" she asked.

"Oh! Nothing!"

"There is something for sure," she said, pouring wine into the glasses.

"Cheers!" I said and took a sip of wine.

Sitting with her with the wine glasses reminded me of that night when Anamika and I were together at my apartment in Mumbai.

"Are you ok?" she asked.

"I guess so."

"You look lost," she said and removed her jacket and stilettos and sat comfortably close to me, her hands touching mine.

"Nothing, it's just that this night reminded me of one of the other nights back in India."

"Must be a good one," she said sipping her wine.

"Yeah, the most beautiful and painful one," I said and finished my wine in one sip.

"Painful? But why? What happened? You can tell me. And don't worry, I am not here to judge you, Kabir."

"No, Kate! There are some painful stories inside my heart which will always remain there. It's a pain that I need to live with. I can't share it with anyone else."

"Well, but people say it's better to share your pain with someone rather than your happiness," Kate said and took the glass from me and kept it on the table. Then, she took my hand and kept it on hers.

"People say many things, but not everything they say is true. Sometimes, time is the best healer and not people," I said and got up from the couch. I picked the wine bottle and started drinking from it directly.

"I think you should stop drinking now," Kate said, coming towards me.

I turned back and looked at her. There she was, smiling again. I could see Anamika standing next to me. I kept looking at her.

"What are you looking at?" she asked.

"Looking at your beautiful eyes," I replied, looking at her. The vision had become very blurry and with the alcohol and dim lights of the room, her face was barely visible.

"Aren't my eyes beautiful!" she asked, taking the wine bottle from me.

"Yes, very beautiful and deep. Anamika, I want to keep looking into your eyes forever," I said, trying hard to keep my eyes open.

"Then, keep looking into it." She came close to me and stood on my feet, her body touching mine. "This night is not going to come back in your life, so let me just take away all your pain for tonight, Kabir." With that, she started opening the buttons of my shirt.

"Where were you for all this while? I looked for you everywhere," I said, sipping wine from the bottle.

"With you, here. In your exquisite suite," she replied and pushed me on the bed.

"You don't know how much I looked for you everywhere, Anamika," I said. My eyes were closed and I could feel her fingers running over my body. "You don't have any idea what I have gone through in life without you. My life cannot be beautiful without you, Anamika."

I was lost in my feelings as I confessed, "I love you. I truly love you. This life is incomplete with you, Anamika."

"I love you, Anamika. I love you."

The next morning, I woke up with a really heavy head. I found it difficult to open my eyes. When I finally opened them to slits and looked at the clock, it was almost noon. The bed was messy and our clothes were lying on the floor. My head started spinning as most of the scenes from last night started playing in front of me.

Oh shit! I pulled my hair.

"I shouldn't have done this. It's all my fault." I cursed myself, thinking about last night. And then, I saw Kate coming towards me.

"Here you go! A strong coffee for you," Kate said as she walked in a bathrobe with two mugs of coffee.

I didn't reply. I really was angry with myself.

She came closer and passed a coffee mug to me.

"What happened? Why aren't you talking to me, my friend?" Kate asked.

"What can I say, Kate? I am not in a condition to speak anything. I am ashamed of myself."

"Ashamed? But why? You were talking a lot last night, then what happened now?" Kate asked, sipping her coffee.

"The guy you met last night wasn't me. I mean whatever happened, I never thought I would ever get into such a thing. This is wrong because—"

"—because there is someone whom you love truly, right? What's her name?" She was thinking. "Ah, some Ana...Ana..." She wanted to pronounce but could not.

"Anamika," I completed.

"Oh yes, Anamika!"

"How do you know her name and how do you know that I love her?" I asked, looking at her.

"Because, my friend, that was the only name you were taking constantly after we went to bed."

"Then?" I asked.

"Then what, you were so high that you kept taking her name and kept saying how much you love her. You were literally pleading her to come back in your life. If that wasn't enough, you were looking up and complaining to god about your destiny. You were telling god to send her back in your life again because you truly love her." Kate said, looking into my eyes.

"Yes, I truly love her. But then, whatever happened between us last night is not right. I am feeling guilty about it now."

"Well, in that case, you don't have to feel guilty at all," she said, taking back the mug from me. "The truth, my friend is that nothing happened between us last night."

"What?"

"Yes, because you kept calling her name and then, at one point, you pushed me away. And then, you passed out. So, nothing happened."

"Really? I don't believe this." There was a spark in my eyes now.

"Yes, really! The whole night you were sleeping on the bed and I was on the couch there," she said, pointing at the couch.

"I must say, you truly love that girl. I have seen many people coming here and crushing their so-called love right here on such beds every night. But you, my friend, are different. I don't know your story, but I will pray to god that she comes back into your life soon."

"Thanks Kate! I am sure she will. It's just a matter of time." I was confident of my love more than ever now.

"For now, it's time for me to leave you alone again. I have to go, my friend," she said while picking up her clothes and went into the washroom. She came out after a quick bath.

"Goodbye, my friend," she said and kissed me on my cheek.

"Hey wait, Kate!" I said. I took out my wallet. "Here!" I said, giving her whatever money I had in my wallet.

"This, for what?" She looked surprised.

"For the lovely time you spent with me last night. For accompanying me and for taking such good care of me, my friend," I replied.

She looked at me for a while and smiled. "Well, in that case, let me tell you that I don't take money to take care of my friends. You are a friend to me now, not some customer."

"But, Kate..." I wanted to speak but she stopped me.

"Do take care of yourself, my friend. And if you feel like meeting a friend again, you know where to find me. Goodbye Kabir!" She smiled.

I bade her goodbye and closed the door behind her. I prepared another cup of coffee for myself and came to the open terrace of the room. I walked towards the end of the terrace. The view was mesmerizing and the breeze was amazing. I placed the coffee mug carefully on the edge of the wall. Then, I pulled a terrace chair close enough to the end of the terrace wall, got on to it and opened my arms to breathe in some fresh air. To breathe in life again.

# 22

## Manali, Himachal Pradesh

I still had a couple of days left before joining work so I went to see Maa.

I flew to New Delhi and then, took a long drive to Manali. After the long journey, I was finally standing in front of my home. I had not informed Maa that I was coming to meet her as I wanted to surprise her and see her reaction.

The house still looked the same, nothing had changed except the trees in the garden which had really grown taller. And also, the fresh paint of the house walls, for which I had convinced Maa on the first Diwali after I started working in Mumbai.

Ours was a beautiful house, with a huge garden in front with some beautiful plants and trees. The house was in between the hills and the best part was the veranda at the back. The veranda faced the valley directly, with an uninterrupted view of the mountain ranges.

I stood outside the house for a while, remembering the time I had spent playing around in the garden. How I used to make Maa run behind me when she used to force me to take a bath during winters.

It was almost evening when I entered the house. As expected, Maa was having tea in the veranda.

I walked slowly towards her and said, "Maa."

She turned back quickly, looked at me and kept looking. She could not believe her eyes that I was standing in front of her. I am sure she was in a happy shock. She froze where she was standing and just smiled at me. We both kept looking at each other and then, I saw tears rolling down her eyes. I walked closer and hugged her.

"Kabir, my son! Is that really you?" she said slowly. I could see she was still crying.

"Yes, Maa. It's me," I replied, wiping her tears.

"Oh Kabir! Good that you came. I was really missing you, my son."

"I missed you too, Maa. And that's why I am here."

She didn't speak again for some time and kept looking at me. No questions about my sudden visit to Manali, no queries about my work. Nothing. I could make out that she was overwhelmed with emotions upon seeing me.

"Maa, will you stop looking at me like this and cook something for me? I am really hungry," I said.

That instigated a lot of excitement in her. "Go, take a bath first! You must be tired. I will go and prepare dinner," she replied, picking up her empty teacup.

I picked up my bag and went towards my room.

"Kabir," she said as I was about to enter my room.

"Yes, Maa," I turned back.

"Take a bath with hot water. It's cold here and it's not *your* Mumbai," she taunted me.

"Yes, Maa. I know it's not Mumbai." I smiled back and went inside the room.

I took a hot shower which felt really good, and then I headed to the kitchen to look for Maa.

"Oh wow, gobi ke paranthe!" I sounded excited like a child.

"Yes, your favourite! I am sure you won't be able to resist now?" she asked, changing the side of the parantha.

"Looking at this yummy parantha, who can resist, Maa! I am very hungry now." I chuckled.

"Go, set up the dining table. I would be done in the next two minutes".

I went to set up the dining table. Maa served hot parantha with a bowl of curd, mint chutney and a spoon of her signature homemade mango pickle. The food looked delicious.

"Hmm, this is so yummy, Maa," I said, licking the mint chutney with my finger.

She didn't say anything, but kept looking at me with a smile.

"What? Why are you looking at me like this, Maa?"

"Nothing! Just wondering how on earth, you landed back like this."

"I was missing you, Maa. Then, I thought of giving you a surprise," I replied, avoiding eye contact.

"And?" she asked.

"And, I was missing this home-cooked food," I said, taking another hot parantha from the casserole.

She was looking at me for an appropriate answer and I was still avoiding eye contact. I knew she could look through me.

"Kabir, what's wrong?" she finally asked softly.

"Nothing is wrong, Maa. Why do you think something is wrong? Everything is fine."

"Because I know there is something wrong, otherwise you wouldn't have come home like this."

"I seriously wanted to meet you, Maa. That's all."

"Then, what about these dark circles, this dull face and your eyes? Where has that spark gone? I cannot see that in your eyes anymore. What are you going through, Kabir?"

"That's just because of too much work, Maa," I tried to sound casual.

"Don't lie, Kabir! I am your mother. I know you are hiding something. Tell me, what is it?"

"Please Maa, let me enjoy my food. Let's not discuss anything beyond this," I said, cutting her short because I did not want her to feel the pain I was going through. She had faced enough in life. I couldn't let that happen again because of me.

"Ok, if you don't wish to," she said and started having dinner.

I was too tired because of the long journey and headed to my bedroom, hoping to get a good sleep. I was feeling bad for the kind of response I gave to Maa. I knew she was worried as saw pain in my eyes. But, I didn't want her to know that her son was shattered from within. I didn't want her to know that her son, in whom she took a lot of pride, was putting all the dreams of his life at stake. No, I couldn't let that happen. I had to let this pain be within me. I was here to give her happiness, not my pain.

Since good sleep was like a dream for me now, I tossed in bed the whole night. I slept only for a few hours and then, woke up early morning. When I came out of the room, Maa was still sleeping, so I made a cup of tea for myself and sat in the veranda.

The sun was about to rise. The cool breeze from the valley was cold and the clouds made a second sky below the valley. The only voice that echoed all around, was of the birds which were probably singing their morning raga.

With the sun beginning to rise, the colour of the sky started to change. It looked as if god was a painter, sitting with a paintbrush and playing with colours on an infinite canvas called the sky. I got up, stood on the steps of the veranda and opened my arms to welcome the sun. Yes, I was breathing. I was breathing in life.

# 23

"So, what's the plan ahead?" Maa asked over breakfast.

"Plan as in?" I asked.

"Do you have any plans of getting married or not?"

"It's too early, Maa," I replied.

"I guess this is the right age, Kabir. Look at you! You are well settled in Mumbai now, working in a good company and earning well. What else do you need?"

"Nothing! I don't need anything but I don't feel like getting married right now," I said, sipping the tea.

"But why? Do you want to remain single for the rest of your life?" she said, taking back the cup of tea from me and passing me a glass of milk.

"I don't want to be single, Maa, but I don't want to get married just because I am earning well and settled. Also, I don't want to marry someone whom I don't even know."

"So, whom do you want to get married to?" she asked, looking into my eyes. I again avoided eye contact.

"Met someone?" she asked after a while.

I still did not respond.

"I am asking you, Kabir. Have you already met someone? Do you have anyone in your life?"

"Yes and no," I replied finally. I had to.

"What do you mean 'yes and no'?"

"There is someone who is not there with me."

"Then, where is she?" she asked.

"I don't know," I replied in a dull tone

"What does that even mean?"

"It means nothing, Maa. I don't know where she is. She's gone, far away from my life."

"And that's the reason behind this condition of yours! That's why you are here in Manali." She put the pieces of the puzzle together.

I didn't reply as I did not want to discuss this further.

She understood my silence and did not question anymore. We both sat silently, knowing each other's condition until she broke the silence. "I am glad you came, Kabir. Thanks for the wonderful surprise," she said, getting a bit emotional.

"You don't have to thank me, Maa. I really wanted to see you and be at home, away from the crazy hustle-bustle of Mumbai," I said, picking up my plate.

"I know, Kabir. But because of your progress and your dreams, I am sure Mumbai will be your home and not Manali. I cannot think of any other city that will suit you," she said, following me into the kitchen.

"Yes, but I miss you there. Why don't you shift with me? I will take up a bigger apartment," I said, cleaning the plates.

"I can't even think of leaving this house, especially at this age." She looked at me. "I have spent my entire life here. This house, this place, these people with whom I speak, laugh and cry when you are not around, are my world. It's very difficult to leave everything at this stage, Kabir."

"You and your emotions, Maa!"

"Can't help it, son. That's how my life has been," she said, keeping the remaining items in the refrigerator.

"Ok, I will leave you with your emotions. I am going to take a walk around town. It's been years. Let me see how this place looks like now," I said.

"Go! I am sure you will see a lot of changes here. But, people are still the same, full of emotions, just like your mother," she said and smiled.

After getting ready, I stepped out and started walking towards the main town. Passing through the narrow lanes, I remembered my childhood days when I used to run towards the school every morning. With a heavy school bag on my shoulders, taking various short-cuts and passing through these lanes, I used to reach school just a few seconds before the assembly bell.

I remembered how I used to feel excited about the one-rupee coin Maa used to give me every Friday to buy an ice cream candy.

Life was so simple back then. Me, Maa and our small ways of celebrating those small occasions which used to come once in a while at our doorstep to surprise us.

Thinking about old days, I passed a few shops and reached the main town. Urbanization had taken over our small town. The small independent shops were now replaced with the so-called mini supermarkets. The local items which were once the speciality of our town were now being taken over by global brands.

Roaming around various places in Manali, I didn't realize that it was afternoon already. I was definitely craving for some good local food. I wanted to try my luck and see if the old shop, which served amazing local dishes, was still there or not. I started walking towards the uphill road.

I was looking for that small shop and walking ahead when a voice from behind drew my attention. "Hey, Kabir!"

I turned back and saw a guy who was wearing a hoodie, ripped jeans and big trekking shoes, looking at me. I glanced at him carefully. His height was slightly above average but he had that typical pahadi look. With his beard grown and sunglasses on his eyes, it was difficult to recognize him.

"What? Why are you looking at me like this? Seems like you haven't recognized me?" The guy said as he walked towards me and removed his glasses and hat. Now, his face looked a bit familiar.

"Pavan?" I said after a while.

"Of course, it's me, buddy," he said, coming close to me. "Can't believe you are here!" he said.

Pavan and I were school friends till tenth grade. We used to sit together in the class, play and eat together. Back in those school days, we were buddies. In fact, he was the only friend I had in school.

Pavan's father was a government official. He was very strict about him studying and making a good career. His father had high expectations from him, Detailed instructions for cracking the tough Civil Services Exam was given to Pavan right from his childhood. So, when the tenth results were out, Pavan's father took a transfer to Delhi so that Pavan could join a good school and prepare well for Civil Services in Delhi.

I remembered how he never wanted to leave Manali. He used to often tell me how much he loved these mountains. But I guess, destiny had some other plans for him. More than destiny, I knew his dad had other plans for sure.

After he left for Delhi, we never met. Pavan did not come back from Delhi, not till I finished my studies and shifted to Mumbai.

And now, we were meeting again. And that too in Manali.

Circle of life, I guess. That's what people call it, don't they?

Pavan came forward and hugged me. "What a lovely surprise, Kabir!"

"This surprise is from you, Pavan. I had never imagined I would meet you like this. So good to see you," I said, looking at him.

"Yeah, man! How could I not come back to this place?" He said, opening his arms towards the mountains.

"Came back? What do you mean?" I asked.

"Long story! Tea?" he asked.

"Yes, but after lunch. I am very hungry."

"Great then! I know an amazing place. Let's have lunch and we can talk at length."

I insisted on having local food, but he mentioned a popular café which served good food. I was glad that it was a quiet place, so that we could talk peacefully. It was a beautiful café which was surrounded by the hills. The walls were decorated with amazing pictures of the mountains, rivers and adventures sports. A few of the adventure equipments such as trekking sticks, helmet, and safety harness were kept on the other side of the wall as showpieces. The glass windows which were facing the Himalayan range, took the vibes of the café to a different level.

As we entered, the cashier greeted both of us and signalled to the waiter to take us to the table next to the huge glass window.

"So, what would you like to have?" Pavan asked.

"Anything is fine since I don't know what their specialty is. I'll be fine with whatever you order," I replied, turning the pages of the menu.

Pavan smiled and gave the order without even looking at the menu. I guessed he was a regular visitor.

"Seems like you come here often," I said.

"Yeah, almost daily, if I am not on any trek."

"Trek? I didn't understand. And have you shifted back to Manali for good?" I asked, giving him a surprised look.

"Yes, I have shifted back. This time forever."

"Wow, that's amazing. But what about your father? As far as I remember, he shifted you all from here because he wanted you to prepare for the Civil Services Exams, right? What about that?"

"Oh, yes! We shifted to Delhi just for that. I did prepare for the Civil Services as instructed by him." he said, sipping water.

"Don't tell me you flunked?" I said smiling at him.

"Ha ha! No, it was the other way round, you idiot. I cleared the prelims but then..."

"Then, what? Didn't clear the mains?"

"No! I didn't appear for the mains," Pavan replied.

"But why?" I was surprised by his answer.

"Because that's not what I wanted to do. You know that I loved this place. This is where I belong. I was not meant for any typical 9 to 6 government job. I can't do that."

"But then, what about your future? Career?"

"Career? What's the use of a life when you don't get to enjoy every day. That's not called life; that's called a prison, my friend."

"Philosophy!" I taunted.

"You can say that but I learned this through my experience while I was preparing for the Civil Services. I was doing good in that, but that wasn't giving me any happiness."

"I understand. Tell me, how did you convinced uncle?"

"One day, I gave up and I told dad clearly about my interest of going back to Manali."

The waiter came and served the food in the meantime.

"Did he agree?" I asked, serving food onto my plate.

"You think he would have agreed? But I was clear, so I told him to give me two years to pursue what I wanted to do in life. And then, if I did not succeed, I would do whatever he wanted to me do."

"Wow man! Sounds like a movie. Then what?"

"I knew pretty well what I needed to do in order to return to Manali. That plan had been ready in my mind since years," Pavan winked at me and continued. "So I spent a few months in Dehradun and completed my mountaineering and trekking course. After the course, I went on to complete various treks in the first year and summited a few well-known and dangerous peaks in India and abroad. After that, I returned to Manali."

"Wow! Then?"

"In the first few months, I explored a few new treks between Manali and Ladakh. Then, finally one day, I opened a small independent agency by the name of 'Himalayan Treks and Mountaineering'. Through social media, I started inviting people from India as well as overseas to explore the unexplored mountain treks with me."

"Oh, so you take people on treks and help them explore the beauty of this Himalayan range?"

"Yes, my friend! We are now officially the biggest and the best mountaineering and adventure sports agency. People from around the globe come here and enjoy the untouched and less explored destinations with us. They spend time with these mountains and I ensure that when they leave, they go back with an experience which they cherish for the rest of their lives."

"Amazing!" I said, finishing the food.

"My love for this place remains intact and I also make a decent living out of it. Most importantly, the happiness I get is incomparable," he concluded, looking at the valley.

"I am impressed, Pavan. It's amazing that you're doing what you love. I can see your happiness in your eyes."

"This is my true love, Kabir, and now, even dad has realized this. He is happy, looking at my success."

"Hmm, I am sure he must be very happy."

"All that is fine, but tell me, how come you are here? I mean, you are working in Mumbai, right? I met your mother a few months back in the market."

"I am still working in Mumbai. I am on a break right now. I've been staying away from Maa for too long so I came here to stay with her," I replied. I didn't want to get into any other discussion so I avoided talking about anything else. I told him about my work and my life back in Mumbai, excluding the Anamika part.

"That's great! What a luxurious life you are living! Not many can reach the stage where you have reached in such a short time," he praised me fondly. "I am sure aunty must be very proud of you," he said and signalled to a waiter to clear the table.

"Yes, she takes a lot of pride because I have achieved whatever she had dreamt for me."

"Proud of you, Kabir." he said, looking at me. "Tea?"

"Some other day, man. Maa must be waiting for me at home. I need to go back to her or else she would start complaining about me for not spending time with her," I said and signalled to the waiter to get the bill.

"I understand. After all, you have come all the way here to meet her."

"I think I should leave. Waiter, can you get the bill please?" I finally asked aloud after waiting for a couple of minutes.

"He won't get the bill," Pavan said, walking me till the café gate.

"What do you mean he won't get the bill?" I asked, looking at the cashier.

"Because it's my café!" he replied, smiling.

"What? But you said you have a mountaineering and adventure sports agency."

"Yeah, but we built this café so that people could come here and share their happy adventure stories with their friends and the people they have met here. It makes this place a little special."

"Pavan, I must say that you really are living your dreams to the fullest. Proud of you! I am so happy to meet you again, my friend," I said and patted his back.

"Thanks! By the way, what are you doing tomorrow?" he asked.

"Nothing much, would be at home only," I replied.

"Great! I am taking some tourists for a day trek to a beautiful location. You must come with us, Kabir."

"Not a bad idea, Pavan. But are you sure? I hope your tourists don't mind me joining you."

"Oh no! Not at all. They all are here to explore this little heaven and make new friends. So, it's absolutely perfect," he concluded.

"Done, sir," I said and smiled.

"See you tomorrow at 7:00 a.m. sharp, here at the café."

"All right, I will be here, Pavan. Goodbye for now."

"Goodbye, Kabir."

It was wonderful to meet an old friend. His approach towards life and the story of his love for this place made me smile.

Not many people can do that. It's a tough call to choose between your heart and your mind. One needs to listen to their inner calling, choose and walk on a path which leads to utter satisfaction and happiness. Those who do that can master their life.

# 24

The next day, I reached the cafe at 7:00 a.m. sharp. His team was loading food items and some trekking equipment in an open jeep while Pavan was busy giving instructions and information to a few foreign tourists about the trek. Soon, we got into another open jeep and headed towards the base location of the trek.

After driving for almost an hour, we reached the base location and started trekking. As Pavan had mentioned, he had explored new treks and destinations. Despite being a local, this was an unexplored destination for me as well. The trek involved steep climbing at certain places with the help of a rope, while at a certain location, we even crossed a rock river.

I must say, Pavan and his team were well-equipped with all the necessary safety gears to complete the trek. We also took a couple of breaks when healthy and tasty snacks were served. Pavan was truly an expert of his field; he knew each and every corner of the trek so well.

It was a different experience, connecting with nature again. During one of the short breaks, Pavan asked everyone to keep their cell phones and cameras aside and sit separately to enjoy the spectacular view of the valley without speaking a word with anyone. He instructed everyone to think of the happiest moment of their life and reflect on that. His idea was to make us listen to our heartbeats by disconnecting with the chaotic world we all lived in.

I guess everyone enjoyed the day trek and returned to Pavan's café. It was evening and the sun was about to set. The tourists thanked Pavan and headed towards their hotel.

"How was it?" Pavan asked me after everyone left.

"I can't explain it in words. It was fabulous."

"I am glad that you liked it," he said and smiled.

"Can't thank you enough for this experience, man."

"You don't need to thank me, Kabir. You are my buddy," he said, keeping his hand on my shoulder. "By the way, our tea party is still pending."

"Yeah, I am completely exhausted right now. How about tomorrow?" I replied.

"Sure, let's meet tomorrow evening then," Pavan agreed.

"Great! Will see you here then."

"Not here, Kabir."

"Then?"

"Remember that sunset point behind our school where we used to go?"

"Oh that! Yes. How can I forget that place! No one used to go there, thinking it's a haunted place. But, we both have spent many evenings there," I said.

"People still don't go there much. Let's meet there in the evening and enjoy the sunset like before. What say?" Pavan asked.

"Let's do that," I replied.

I bade him goodbye and reached home to an amazing meal ready at the dining table. That's the thing with mothers; they know what you want even if you don't say a word to them.

After dinner, I decided to call it a night. After months, I slept peacefully, without a worry.

Next evening, I walked through the lonely lane behind the school and reached the sunset point where Pavan and I were supposed to meet that evening. This place, which once used to be full of tourists every evening, was now completely empty. People stopped coming here after an unfortunate incident. A young girl had fallen into the valley from one of the huge rocks on the edge of the cliff and died while enjoying the sunset. The search operation lasted for three days, but they could not find her body.

From that day, the local people started making a lot of stories about that place and called it a 'haunted sunset point'. They believed that since the girl had died watching the sunset, every evening, her spirit came to the same point. They also said that if someone was seen enjoying the sunset, her spirit took that person's life by pushing them into the valley, making it the last sunset of their life. Many such stories circulated in the entire town and people stopped visiting the place out of fear.

Unlike all others, Pavan and I used to come to this point out of curiosity, to see the spirit of that young girl. But nothing of that sort caught our attention. Soon, we realized that all those stories were fictional. But since, we wanted to have the place to ourselves, we never went back and told the truth to anyone.

After years, I was again standing on one side of the point where Pavan and I used to sit on huge rocks and enjoy talking for hours. I was looking at the sky, remembering our old school days and the fun we had back then. I was lost in my thoughts when I saw a girl on the other side of the point, standing on the edge of a huge rock.

Seems like people had started coming to this place, I thought, looking at the girl. Her face wasn't visible as she was facing the valley. She had kept her hair open and wore a woollen stole and a full-length skirt.

I looked around to see if anyone was there with her. But to my surprise, she seemed all by herself. There was still time for the sun to set and I could see her clearly. Gradually, she removed her stole and opened her arms towards the sky. It felt as if she was telling the winds to come and hug her. It felt as if she was breathing in life. It instantly reminded me of Anamika.

I kept looking at her, and then at one point, my eyes got stuck on her skirt. It looked similar to the one that I had gifted Anamika that day in Mumbai before going to Siddhivinayak temple.

Anamika! My mind started racing. No no, she couldn't be here. But then, that skirt?

Anyone could buy such a skirt, my mind gave an answer. She was still looking at the sky with her arms open.

I stepped down from the rock and walked a bit towards her to have a closer look. I looked at her carefully this time; her hair were similar to Anamika's, she had the same height. But what grabbed my attention was the way she was standing. With her arms open towards the sky, I could see that she was definitely breathing in life, like Anamika used to do. Her posture was exactly the same as Anamika's.

My heart started beating faster. Somewhere in my heart, I knew that the girl standing there was Anamika. My mind and heart were in a tussle, not able to decide whether it really could be my Anamika or not. I realised that the only way to stop this battle was to actually go and see that girl once. So, I started walking towards her slowly.

I was now only a few steps away from her. I looked at her skirt once again. It was the same skirt which I had gifted to Anamika. I was absolutely sure now. I smiled and kept my hand on my heart, trying to tame my racing heartbeats a little. Finally, she was there! It was going to be the best time of my life again.

I gathered my strength and called out her name. "Anamika!" I said softly.

Probably, she was lost, looking at the beautiful sky and didn't turn, so I called her name again, this time a bit louder.

"Anamika, it's me."

The girl in front of me turned slowly towards me and I could not believe my eyes. She was Anamika! A shiver ran through my body. The girl I had been waiting to meet for such a long time was standing right in front of me.

Though Anamika was standing at a distance, I could clearly see sadness on her face. She neither smiled nor reacted. She kept looking at me without saying a word. Her eyes indicated her immense pain, the scars on her face were screaming of the suffering she might have gone through since the time I met her last.

I was about to walk towards her. But before I could do so, she signalled at me to stand where I was.

"Anamika, it's me Kabir. Don't you recognize me?" I asked.

"Kabir, how can I not recognize you?" she said softly.

"Thank god, Anamika. We finally meet. You don't know how my life has been since you left me that night in Mumbai with this letter," I said, taking out the letter from my pocket.

I was about the take a step towards her when she said, "Don't come near me. Please stop there, Kabir."

"What's wrong with you, Anamika? Why are you stopping me?"

"Because I don't want you to enter my life again, Kabir."

"You don't want me to? But why, Anamika?"

"I don't want you in my life so that I don't go through the pain once again," she said, her tone a bit louder this time.

"Pain! Because of me? What are you saying, Anamika?" I said and tried walking up to her.

"I told you not to come closer to me. Stay there, Kabir!" she shouted on top of her voice.

"Ok! I won't move an inch, but don't say that I am the reason behind your pain," I said, pleading to her.

"Yes, you are, Kabir. I was doing fine before I met you and was slowly coming out of depression. I was happy the way I was breathing life and the way I was living without any support, but then..." She stopped.

"Then what, Anamika? The time that we had spent together, wasn't that amazing? For me, that was the most beautiful time of my life. It was because you were there with me," I said.

"Yes, it was beautiful, Kabir. But, you knew that I had a different battle to fight on my own, without anyone's support. When I left that day, I couldn't handle the pain of leaving you like that. In that short time, I had started enjoying your company. The way you made me happy was really beautiful." She broke down now. "Before meeting you, I was happy with my life. I knew that one day, I would get over my past sufferings and lead a fulfilling life. And then, this other pain of going away from you got unbearable."

"Then why did you leave me like that, Anamika?" I asked.

"Because I knew you would end up spoiling your life too, Kabir. I was going through a phase where I didn't want anyone else to suffer because of my condition," Anamika screamed.

"Spoiling my life? Then, you don't know what my condition has been after you left me that night," I said. "You don't know what all I have done to find you. You don't know the sufferings and the pain that I have gone through, Anamika. All those struggles were because I truly loved you." This time, a tear rolled down from my eyes. "With your absence in my life, I started living your life. Look at me! I have become you, Anamika," I said and fell on my knees.

It was dark now and we were still talking to each other from a distance.

"I loved you too, Kabir. I was dying to be with you. But, this isn't going to last forever."

"Why do you think it's not going to last?" I asked, looking at her.

"Because you only have a clue of what my life is; you only know what I have told you. You don't know my real condition. You haven't seen the other side of my life," she said and continued. "No one would ever spend his life with me after knowing the whole truth, Kabir."

"Who are you to decide that? You just know about yourself, not about what the other person wants," I said, getting up again.

"So, you think that you know me completely? That too, in just a day or probably a night?" she asked.

"You don't need years to know a person, Anamika. Whatever little time we had spent together was sufficient for me. I have decided to make up my mind to spend the rest of my life with you. And, you love me too. What else do we want?"

"My world is different, Kabir. I don't want you to enter it just because you love me. When you see the other side of me, you would leave midway. I can't take that pain, Kabir."

"But why would I leave you, Anamika?"

"Because our paths are different. Our worlds are different. And most importantly, it's not in our destiny to be together," Anamika replied. "I can't let this pain destroy my world. I am already feeling the pain of not having you with me, but I can't be selfish. I can't give you my pain, Kabir. I can't destroy your life too," Anamika explained.

"But I really want to take away all your pain, Anamika. Don't you get it? That's the best way to end all your sufferings," I pleaded.

"Share my pain with you so that you too stop living your life? No, Kabir! That's not the way to end all this."

"Then, how do you want to end all this, Anamika?" I shouted. "Trust me, being together is the only way. Come, hold my hand and start a new journey," I said and extended my hand towards her.

"I am sure there will be someone who will complete this journey with you, Kabir. But it is not me."

"But Anamika—" I was interrupted.

"For now, I know how all this is going to end. I know how to end my pain and sufferings," she said.

"How?" I asked.

This time, she smiled and said, "I knew I would find you here, in Manali, someday. I wanted to see you for the last time so that there are no regrets later," Anamika said. "I came here to breathe in life. I waited for you to come so that I would see your face and bid goodbye to you forever. That way, you won't live with the hope of meeting me again and move on to live a life that you deserve."

"Bid goodbye? What are you saying, Anamika? Please don't leave me! I can't live without you."

"Goodbye, Kabir. I am going to end all my sufferings and pain today," she stated and took a step back towards the edge of the rock.

"Anamikaaa! What are you trying to do?" I shouted in despair.

"Ending my sufferings and going to a world where there is only happiness," she said, standing on the edge of the cliff.

"Don't, please don't do this, Anamika! We will build a different world, full of love and happiness where there will be no place for any sadness or pain. There will be just you and me, I promise."

She didn't respond, but kept smiling as she took another step back.

"I promise I will always keep you happy, till my last breath. Please don't move any further, Anamika," I pleaded. "Don't run away. Come back, Anamika," I said and ran towards her.

"Kabir, being together in this life is not in our destiny. Goodbye, Kabir," she said. She turned towards the cliff and jumped into the valley.

"Anamikaaaaaaa!"

# 25

"Anamikaaa!" I screamed and sat up in my bed, shocked. I opened my eyes and realized that I had tears in my eyes. I was drenched in sweat. In that cold weather too, not just my face, but my whole body was sweating and my heartbeat raced like never before.

The window of my room was wide open and the wind made a scary noise, clashing with the window pane. I glanced through every corner and found myself in my bedroom, all alone.

Oh my god, I had the worst nightmare of my life.

I comforted myself and picked up a glass of water from the bedside table. I looked at the clock. It was almost morning. I drank some water, got up from my bed and walked towards the window. It was so cold outside that I could feel the cool breeze hitting my face. I stood next to the window, thinking about Anamika. Soon, the first ray of light filled the room. With the morning rays, slowly the darkness of the room drifted away. I stood there, waiting for the light that could take away the darkness from my life too.

After the nightmare, I was really scared of going to the sunset point to meet Pavan. But then, I told myself that it was just a dream and went anyway. Pavan had already reached there and was waiting for me. We sat on the rocks near the edge of the cliff. Nobody was there, except both of us. Pavan took out the thermos and filled two cups of tea.

"Here is your tea, Mr Kabir," he said, passing me a cup.

I didn't say anything. I just took the cup from him and stared towards the sky.

As the sunset began, the colours of the sky started changing. God had started spreading colours on this huge canvas once again.

"Hey, what happened? Is everything okay?" Pavan asked. after observing me for a while.

"I am... I am alright, Pavan," I replied in a dull tone.

"Doesn't look like it. What's going on?" he asked again.

"Nothing, really," I replied.

"C' mon, you can tell me. I promise whatever it is, it's going to be a secret between us, just like this place," Pavan said and smiled at me.

"I am just seeking some answers and are not able to get them," I said, after having a sip.

"What answers?" he asked.

"Answers to find myself, my life again," I replied.

"Hmmm. A girl?" he asked.

I didn't reply but he understood my silence.

"I knew there was something going on. It shows in your eyes, Kabir. I noticed it yesterday also, which is why I asked you to come along with me for tea after the trek. I wanted you to open up so you could feel better after sharing it with a friend," Pavan said.

"Thank you Pavan, but it's my battle and I have to fight this alone. No one can help me," I replied. "And, what did you notice yesterday? The whole day we were on a trek and nothing happened that could make you notice any difference," I said.

Pavan smiled, took a sip of tea and continued. "Though you never said anything, I noticed something while we took that short break where I asked everyone to connect with themselves. Remember that part of the trek?"

"Of course, I remember. So?" I asked.

"I noticed that there was something bothering you. It felt as if you were in too much pain and were searching hard for some answers," Pavan said. "On every trek, I have been taking this one particular short break and have seen true happiness in people's eyes after it," Pavan said.

"I was happy too. I mean, it felt really good sitting there, looking at the open sky. It was nice," I said

"But then, you weren't breathing life my friend. I could make that out by just looking at you. There is a difference between living life and breathing life."

"Of course, I was breathing life. How could I not? And I know the difference very well, Pavan," I said, getting a bit irritated.

"Okay okay, if you say so," he said, sipping his tea.

We both were silent for a few seconds until, a few words that Pavan had spoken stumped my mind. I turned towards him. "Hey Pavan! From whom did you hear these words 'breathing life'? How do you know about this?" I asked, looking at him.

"Why? Why do you want to know? These are just words." He shrugged.

"I know these are just words, but tell me. Have you read these words somewhere or have you heard it somewhere, from someone maybe?" I asked.

He kept his cup aside carefully and said, "Frankly, I never knew these words and never had any idea what 'breathing life' meant. But I met someone around two or three months back who taught me and explained its true meaning," Pavan replied.

"Who? Whom did you meet? Where? Please tell me," I said, getting excited.

Pavan looked at me, astonished at the way I reacted. He thought for a while and began speaking. "I remember I was on a trek with a group of tourists and we must have reached halfway at a point from where the view was spectacular. So I asked everyone to take a break. Everyone was just enjoying the view, clicking photographs and selfies, but there was this girl who walked towards the cliff and stood with her arms open, facing the deep valley. It looked weird to me because while others were capturing this beautiful view through those digital lenses, this girl was different from others and that caught my attention."

"Then? Then what happened?" I asked, my eyes sparkling.

"I went up to her. She was still standing with her arms open towards the sky, and was smiling. I asked her what she was up to and she told that she was breathing in life. I asked her how one could breathe life."

"Then, what did she say?" I said, smiling at Pavan. I knew the answer already; I just needed a confirmation.

"She told me that nowadays people are just running in every possible direction. They run behind money, a successful career, fame and many other things. In a quest to do so, they forget to breathe in life.

"She told me that breathing life is nothing but finding true happiness and celebrating little joys of our life. Breathing life is nothing but, smiling without a reason by keeping the worries away and trusting our dear ones," Pavan continued, with a smile on his face.

"She asked me, what's the point of having lots of money if we did not have time for ourselves! Breathing life is to understand the true emotions that we have for ourselves and for others. Most importantly, breathing life is living and enjoying every moment." He looked at me, smiling weirdly and concluded, "I was very impressed with the way she had explained the whole thing. She even helped me breathe life like her."

"How did she do that?" I prodded.

"She asked me to remove my jacket. Then, she made me stand by the cliff, facing the valley with my arms open to welcome the cool breeze. She asked me to reflect back on my own life and think of happy moments. She asked me to connect with this beautiful nature and feel my own heartbeat."

"So, did it make you smile then?" I asked.

"It made no sense to me, but she insisted. Trust me! When I was standing with my arms open, feeling the cold breeze, listening to my own heartbeats and connecting with myself, to my surprise, I was smiling. I was actually breathing life," Pavan said, finishing his tea. "She was a different girl. Very different from the crowd," Pavan concluded.

"I know! She is very different from others," I acknowledged.

"You know?" Pavan was surprised. "What was her name... I forgot?" Pavan asked, trying to remember her name.

"Anamika," I replied, smiling at him.

"Yes... Anamika! But how do you know that girl, Kabir?" He asked and then, looked at me. I was sad again. "Oh, I see! This pain, this sadness, it's because of her, right? And those answers that you were talking about, it's all about Anamika. Am I correct?"

"Yes, Pavan. I love her."

"But does she love you?"

"Of course, she loves me too. I have seen it in her eyes."

"You love her and she also loves you. Then, what's the problem? Why aren't you guys together. Why all this pain, this suffering?" Pavan asked, looking at me.

I didn't reply and he understood my silence. I didn't want to share the other part of the story.

"Kabir, my friend, I know there is more to this story and it's absolutely fine if you don't want to share it with me. I understand your condition. But what I am unable to understand is that if you really love her so much, then why don't you just go and tell her? Make her yours forever. What's stopping you?"

"She is gone away from my life," I replied.

"Gone? Where?" he asked.

"I wish I knew, Pavan. It's been months and I really don't know where she has gone, leaving behind no clue for finding her," I concluded.

Pavan kept looking at me. I knew he must be wondering why I had no clue of where Anamika could be.

"So, it means you absolutely don't have any clue of where she is now?" Pavan asked.

"No, no clue at all. Otherwise we would have been together by now," I said.

Pavan was sad now. We both sat quietly for a while.

"Damn, man...that fire! Else..." he said, banging his feet.

"Fire! What fire?" I asked.

Pavan looked at me. "We take information like address, contact details, emergency point of contact of every tourist coming with us for treks or adventure sports," Pavan explained. "You know, just in case there's an emergency or any kind of casualty, this information can be very useful. We maintain such records." Pavan said.

"Do you have her details?" I said, looking at him hopefully.

Pavan said, keeping his hand on my shoulder, "Last month, there was a huge fire in my office and everything was destroyed in a matter of hours. There was nothing left in our office."

"Oh my god!"

"Sorry, Kabir. I wish I could help," Pavan said in a dull tone.

"Don't be sorry, my friend. It's not you. It's someone called god who doesn't want us to be together. Guess Anamika was right. Maybe it's not in our destiny," I said, throwing a stone above in the sky.

"Don't say that, Kabir! I am sure you both will be together soon. Trust me, that day is not that far."

We had been sitting there for a long time. Eventually, it was time to head back home. Pavan was driving his jeep and I was sitting beside him. We were quiet. I guess both of us were thinking about Anamika.

We passed through the narrow lanes and reached the market. It was dark and there was hardly anyone on the road. The shops were closed in the market and people had gone back home to spend time with their families. We were reaching the end of the market road when Pavan suddenly stopped his jeep.

"What happened?" I asked.

He didn't say anything and reversed the jeep immediately, stopping outside a tourist office.

"What happened? Why have you stopped here? The shop is closed now," I said, pointing at the shutter.

"Because I think I know where Anamika would have gone from here," Pavan said, looking at me.

"What! Where?" I said, getting hopeful again.

"There!" He pointed at the board on top of that tourist office which read 'Trip to Ladakh Monasteries'.

"Ladakh monasteries?" I looked at Pavan and then thought for a while. "Are you sure she was headed to Ladakh from here?" I asked.

"Yes, Kabir. I am sure because I still remember that after the trek, when I was bidding goodbye to everyone, I had asked her about her next destination," Pavan recalled.

"Then, she said Ladakh?" I asked.

"She told me that after Manali, she was going to spend a few days in a Buddhist monastery in Ladakh. I found it strange because no tourist had ever talked about spending days in a monastery, and that too in Ladakh."

"Then, what happened?"

"Nothing, I offered her our agency's services, but she kept saying that she was going to be there all alone and since she was planning to spend time in a monastery, she didn't need any further help."

"Yes, she prefers to be alone. I want to hold her hand and pull her out of loneliness," I said.

I kept looking at the board for some time. My heart asked me to go and look for her, but my mind said it would be another failed attempt. I kept thinking about her. Finally, I looked at Pavan.

"Can you help me reach Ladakh, Pavan?" I asked, after thinking for a while. "You have helped me a lot, but I don't have time. I need to be back in Mumbai by next week. Before I go back, I need to find Anamika. I need to find those answers. Please help me."

He thought for a while, looked at his watch and said, "You still have time, Kabir. You can take an early morning flight to Leh. Will that work?" Pavan asked.

"Of course it will work. Let's go," I said, looking at him.

"Great! I will arrange a car for you at the Leh airport. The driver will take you to all the places," Pavan said, starting the jeep.

"I don't know how to thank you, buddy," I said, getting a bit emotional.

"You don't need to. I wish I could have come with you, but—"

"But, it's my battle, Pavan. I have to fight and win it on my own," I said.

# 26

I took an early morning flight to Leh and landed a couple of hours later, with a hope to find Anamika.

Pavan had already arranged a cab for me. He had instructed the driver to take me to the monasteries.

"Which monastery do you wish to go to, sir?" the cab driver asked, taking my bag from my hand.

"All of them," I replied

"Sure sir," he said, keeping my bag in the car.

Ladakh is full of peaceful monasteries. People from all over the world come here to experience its serenity, and also in search of peace.

I was here in search of someone who could be the reason for my peace.

For the next four days, I visited almost each and every monastery, looking for Anamika everywhere. But, with so many travellers coming to the place, and with no photographs and other details of her, it really was an impossible task to find her.

I also described her appearance to a few local residents and shop owners to check if they had seen someone similar in their area, but that also did not work. With each passing day, I was getting restless. I felt her near me, but wasn't able to see her in front of my eyes.

"It's been four days and still no clue of her," I murmured to myself, holding a bowl of hot thukpa.

The sun was about to set and the bikers were returning to their base camp and hotels. I saw couples holding hands, laughing, and enjoying the serene beauty of the place. They looked so happy.

"We would have enjoyed our life like this, if you hadn't left me. Life would have been really different, Anamika. But now, it is of no use," I said to myself, thinking about her.

"Sir, can we go now?" the driver said, collecting the bowl from me

"Do we have any other monastery left to be visited?" I asked.

"Hmm... not really, sir. We have covered almost every monastery around this area," he replied.

"Except one," he said, suddenly.

"Which one?" I asked

"That one," he said, pointing at a huge monastery on a very high hill.

"It is a Buddhist monastery and the biggest one, sir. That is the only one left," he said.

Though the monastery was very far, but still, because of its really huge structure, I could see it clearly.

Looking at the monastery, my heart leapt with joy. I was sure I was going to find her there.

"Then, let's go there!" I said.

"We can leave early morning tomorrow, sir. We will reach there by afternoon that way," the driver said.

"Why not right now?" I asked

"Sir, it is very far from here. We cannot reach there today. On top of it, it's almost evening and travelling at night is not advisable," the driver concluded.

"I don't have time. We have to leave now," I said, walking towards the car.

"Sir, it's not safe," he requested again.

"I will pay you extra, please," I said.

He had been with me for four days and probably understood the reason for my coming there. He knew that I was searching for someone. He could sense that I was upset at not finding her anywhere.

Looking at my face and my condition, he agreed to come; not because of the money I was paying him, but because he really wanted to help me find her. Soon, we again began our journey.

# *Inside the monastery*

## Present Day

"That's how I reached here in search of her," I said, walking towards the monk, who was sitting next to the fireplace, listening to my story.

"And she had told me that if it is written in our destiny, then we would definitely meet. Otherwise, just think of it as one of the stories of your life and move ahead," I repeated the last lines of the letter she had written to me. I took out the letter from my pocket and passed it to the monk.

The monk took the letter, but didn't read it. He kept it aside.

"How can I move ahead when I know that I love her? When I know that we are destined to be together? Why am I not able to find her? Why aren't we together? Didn't she love me?" I was agitated.

"No one knows the answers better than you," he replied, pointing at the letter.

"Answers? But, I really don't have any," I said.

"You said that you don't want to move ahead because you love her. That's your first realization and your answer," the monk said and smiled as I looked at him. "Many people do not even realize what love means. They fail to understand it," he continued. "But here you are! You have realized what it means to you. You truly love her and that's your biggest strength, my son."

He smiled at me lovingly, saying, "So what if she is not around you! What's more important is that you love her. I think you need to believe in the power of love. If you truly love someone, then one day, a miracle will happen and your beloved will be there in front of you."

"But why did she leave me like this?" I asked.

"That's again because of love, my son. Love in which she doesn't want her past to come between you and her in the future," the monk spoke again. "She was scared of losing you in the future, so before you could get more attached to her, she left you. Perhaps, hoping that you would come out of this situation before it's too late. She sacrificed her emotions and that's true love, son," he explained.

"It would not have been easy for her to leave. But, just because she loved you, she thought of not creating more troubles in your life. That's why she took the pain and moved away from your life," he concluded.

"Such a foolish girl!" I said.

"Love makes you do such foolish things, Kabir. Look at yourself!" He said softly.

I looked at him intently as he explained, "Aren't you here, doing some foolish stuff in the middle of the night? What would have happened if I had not heard your voice? Did you think about it? he asked.

"No, you didn't! Because at that time, you did what you thought was right. Just like that, she also did what was right for both of you according to her," the monk explained. "Neither you nor she is right or wrong because love knows no such boundaries. It is simply love."

Hearing his words, for the first time after months, I understood the true definition of love. I had a smile on my face.

"I love her. She loves me. But, what about our destiny? Aren't we supposed to be together?" I asked.

"If you both love each other truly, then you don't have to go anywhere to find her. Destiny will ensure your togetherness. You just have to keep loving her and wait until fate makes things possible for both of you," he said.

"So, what should I do now?" I asked.

"Go back, Kabir! Start living your life. Keep her memories in your heart and keep loving her. Don't ever doubt your belief and your love. Don't ever think that you are not going to find her. Why cry, when you know that you both love each other? It is only a matter of time and I am sure this will pass soon," he told me. "Don't search her any further because she is there with you all the time. Similarly, you are with her all the time," he said, pointing at my heart.

"It is not about loving a person when he or she is in front of your eyes, but loving each other all the time, even when that person is not with you," the monk continued.

"Hmm." It made sense to me.

"Love is not a phase which will pass. It is an entire life which you should be enjoying each day, each minute, till the time you take your last breath," he concluded. "So, go back! I am sure you both will be together one day. And, that day is not very far."

His words comforted me and I really had some positive vibes running through my mind and heart. I got up from my place and walked towards the monk who was now standing near the window.

"Thank you very much," I said.

"For what?" He looked at me and asked.

"For guiding me towards the right path of life and for making me understand the deeper meaning of love. I think god wanted me to come here to understand and feel this. That's why he created this situation and separated us," I said, looking up towards the sky from the window.

"But now, I know what true love means. I am sure god will make a path so that I can reach her and get her back into my life," I concluded.

"He will son, he will," he said.

"Thank you once again."

"God bless both of you."

I took his blessings and came out of the monastery. The dark night was over now. I could see the first rays hitting the mountain tops. I felt as if I had been reborn with lots of positivity.

Soon, I was heading back to Mumbai, but with a real smile after long. Inside my heart, I knew that I was going to meet her. After speaking with the monk the previous night, I was sure that we were destined to be together. I knew, sooner or later, we would meet one day. But when? This time, I knew that destiny would answer that question for me.

# 27

## *Anamika*

Dr Neha was looking at my recent medical reports which I had received last night. Though, it was just a matter of a few hours till I could see her, but it was the longest night. I read my reports twice, thrice and multiple times. Every time I looked at the reports, there was only one question that arose in my mind. 'What now?'

It had been a few months since I returned from Mumbai. But, not even a single day had passed when I had not thought about Kabir and the time that I had spent with him. I felt like going back to him so many times, but just couldn't gather the courage to face him. Especially, after the night when I left him all alone, with just a letter.

Dr Neha finished going through my reports, came back to her chair and kept my records on her desk. She kept looking at me for a while, and then finally, she spoke after a sigh. "No, I can't let you jump into this, especially after knowing what you are going through and your condition." She stopped and thought again. "No, I don't suggest you take such steps," Dr Neha finally instructed.

"But Dr Neha, I have thought about it. I guess, that's where destiny is taking me," I said.

"Please try and understand that you are not only my patient, but also a dear friend. As a friend, I suggest you rethink your decision. You still have some time."

That was true. Ever since I had returned from the US, Dr Neha not only played the role of a good doctor, but we had bonded well. At a very young age, she had made a mark for herself, not only as a good doctor but also as a humble person, who was always ready to go beyond the call of duty to serve people. As a doctor and a friend, she was aware of my condition and knew what I was going through.

"Time! Knowing my situation, you really think I have time, Dr Neha?" I said, pointing at the medical reports. "I have been running away from myself for years. From my life and from everyone. You also know the reasons behind it very well. But now, when I don't want to run away anymore, you are asking me to rethink my decision? I said, looking at her. "No, Dr Neha! I am not going to run away now," I said,while collecting my medical reports.

"Why don't you understand? I know what has been going on in your mind since the time you have returned from Mumbai. I completely understand and respect your feelings but... this is different. You need to understand the criticality," Neha said, sounding concerned this time.

"I know the criticality. I have thought over it and I am going to face it, Dr Neha."

She sighed and said, "I guess you are not going to listen to my advice this time." I could see the disappointment in her eyes. "But if you have decided, why don't you go back to Kabir? What's the point of controlling your feelings to such an extent? And, that too, after knowing that you love him? I think he loves you too."

"He definitely loves me, Dr Neha. I have seen true love in his eyes. The way he made me feel so special in just one day, it couldn't be anything but love," I replied.

"Then, for god's sake, go back to him. Please. You know you don't have much time now," Dr Neha almost shouted.

"Go back to him? And destroy his life too? Is that what you want me to do?" I said, getting up from my chair. "You are my doctor. My condition is not hidden from you. You know what I have been going through all my life," I said agitatedly.

"That's exactly what my point is. You need true love in your life. And, with love, anything can be healed. Moreover, when you know he also loves you so much, what is stopping you from going back to him?"

"My fear, Dr Neha."

"Fear? What sort of fear?"

"My fear of not giving him the love that he deserves in his life. My fear of losing him in my life because of my condition," I said. "He has his entire life ahead of him. He has his dreams to achieve. And most importantly, he deserves someone much better than me, who can support him and hold his hand for the rest of his life," I explained.

Dr Neha got up from her chair and walked towards me. "Why can't you be that person who can support him?"

"Me? And support?"

"Yes, why not!" she said, coming close to me.

"A person who herself requires support all the time, not sure where her life is heading. You think she can be someone's support? Never, Dr Neha!"

"Oh! Why don't you understand! It's time now. Now, after these reports, you know what's going to happen. Trust me, you need him now—"

I did not let her speak any further. "I have always followed your advice, Dr Neha. And done whatever you had asked me to do. But this time, I am sorry, I am going to do what I feel is right for me," I said, collecting my bag.

"Listen to me! It's going to be a tough journey ahead. Please listen to me," Dr Neha said, keeping her hand on my shoulder.

"I know that the journey ahead is tough. But, that's the only way left for me. After this journey, I am going to see the light on the other side of life."

Dr Neha didn't say anything. She just kept looking at me. I walked towards the door and then, turned towards her. "You know what, Dr Neha. Sometimes, this so-called pain and such tough journeys are the most beautiful journeys of life. Once you complete the journey, there is no space for any kind of pain, sadness and regrets. I want to be on the other side now and this is the only way," I conveyed my decision.

"Goodbye, Dr Neha," I said and closed the door behind me.

# 28

## *Kabir*

"Hey Shruti, when is the client meeting scheduled?" I asked, standing near her cubicle. I had resumed office this morning after a break as suggested, or rather instructed, by Mr Taneja.

I had shaved after months. My face looked fresh because I had slept well after months.

"Kabir, you are back from the break!" She was delighted to see me.

"Yes, I am."

"Great! So, where all have you been?" she asked.

"Ladakh," I replied

"Ladakh... to find her?"

"Yes." I smiled.

"Did you?" She jumped up in excitement.

"No! But I found myself," I replied.

She smiled.

"And soon, I will find her too," I said, winking at her.

"Wow! Seems like our Kabir is back!" Shruti said.

"Back with a bang! Tell Mr Taneja that we are going to crack every deal from now on. And, give me the details of the upcoming meetings please," I said.

"We have quite a few meetings lined up in the months to come, Kabir." Shruti handed over the client list.

"Don't worry, we will get every deal closed. Leave it to me," I said confidently.

"Now that you are back, I am sure we will. Oh Kabir! I am so happy for you," Shruti said and hugged me.

I worked really hard to concentrate on my work and the campaigns that had been assigned to me. However, Taneja did not give me any big campaigns as he still had doubts about my confidence.

Even though those were smaller campaigns, for the next five months, I did not see whether it was day or night. I constantly worked hard so that I could get every deal closed in our favour. More than the deal, I wanted to prove myself again.

As far as Anamika was concerned, not even a single day passed without me thinking about her. Now, rather than thinking why she left me like this, I used to think about the good time we had spent together.

Each day, I used to pass by the café where I had met Anamika in Mumbai. And instead of getting upset, I used to remember and cherish the time we both had spent there. I kept my hopes high as I knew I was going to meet her one day, for sure.

Days passed and turned into months. It'd been five months since my return from the break. I was trying hard to prove myself again. On one such day, when I was leaving from office, a voice drew my attention near the elevator.

"Hey, Kabir!"

I looked back and saw Yamini smiling at me.

"Long time, Kabir," she said, walking towards me.

"Yes, long time, but what a surprise! How come you are here in the office, Mrs Taneja?" I asked and spoke formally as there were still many people in the office.

"You know Mr Taneja does not have time for me at home, so I thought I would meet him here. But as usual, he is busy in some meeting," she replied.

"Yes, he has some visitors today."

"Stop covering for him, Kabir. I know he is your boss, but don't forget I am your friend." She winked as we waited for the lift to open.

We entered the lift and since there were a couple of more people, we did not talk much.

"So, where are you heading to?" she asked as soon as we reached the ground floor.

"I am going home," I replied.

"So early?" she said, looking at her watch.

"Yeah, I am kind of tired, hence leaving early today," I replied.

"Can you spend some time with me, Kabir?" she asked.

"But Mrs Taneja..."

"Just over a coffee, Kabir. Please?" She insisted and I could not say no.

We reached a nearby café in our own separate cars.

"What is wrong with you, Kabir?" she asked, when we were sitting inside the café.

"Wrong with me? Nothing," I said.

"I heard Mr Taneja talking to someone that he was still sceptical about giving you big assignments. He was also saying that you are still recovering." Yamini looked into my eyes and told me. "In the past couple of months, you have not turned up for any parties at home too. I tried calling you on your number, but you never responded. I hope everything is ok?" She sounded concerned.

"Things were a little different back then. Whatever you heard about me was correct. But now, everything is alright. I am back," I replied, passing her a cup of coffee.

"I am glad that you are back, but what had happened?"

"Hmm... long story. I will tell you some other day," I said to avoid the topic.

"But Kabir..." she wanted to ask further, but I changed the topic.

"You tell me, how's your life going?" I asked.

"My life? What do you think? It has become hell now."

"Why, what happened?" I asked. It wasn't a surprise. I already knew what she was going through.

"As if you don't know anything!" she replied, looking into my eyes.

"I know Yamini, but he is your—"

"Husband, right? A husband who is never there for me," she replied.

"But whatever he is doing is for you," I said, taking Mr Taneja's side.

"For me?" she asked.

"Yes, of course! For you and your happiness," I said.

"Can you buy happiness and love with money?" she asked.

"I know money can't buy all that, but if you want to make things work positively between you and him, instead of complaining and cribbing over it, go and have a word with him," I said.

"Do you think he has time for that?" she almost chuckled sadly.

"You have to make him understand, Yamini. You both are life partners and you both are very lucky that the person you love is there in front of your eyes. You just have to make an effort to push things back on track," I said.

"You think I haven't tried, Kabir? I have. Many times. But, because I don't get any response from him, I have given up now."

"How can you give up so easily, Yamini? That too for your soul mate? You both have chosen each other. You have spent so many beautiful years together. You have created so many memories together! And now, because of some silly issues, you are saying that you have given up?" I literally blasted.

"You have always talked about your problems with Mr Taneja. Have you ever tried asking what his concerns are with you? Maybe, he has something in his heart which he is not telling you. That could be one of the reasons that this distance between both of you has increased so much," I asked.

"Kabir..."

"No, Yamini. Please don't ever talk about giving up on your relationship. It's a gift and people are lucky if they get to enjoy this gift together," I said. "Look at me, Yamini! I am not as lucky as you are. You wanted to know what happened to me. Then, listen to this carefully. Maybe then, you would understand the value of relationships and realize how lucky you both are."

I narrated my entire story to her over that cup of coffee. She listened to everything with undivided attention. By the time I finished my story, I could see tears rolling down from her eyes.

"Oh Kabir! I never knew you have gone through so much in the past few months. I am really sorry."

"Sorry for what, Yamini? I have not lost hope of meeting her. I know she loves me and I love her too. It's just a matter of time. One day, if it is written in our destiny, we would definitely meet," I concluded.

"I am sure you will be together soon," she said.

"We will. But for now, don't waste your time over all these things. Life is beautiful only if we have our soul mate beside us. Don't think of letting him go anywhere. Go, win him back. So what, if he is busy with work! Make him fall for you again. Talk to him and make him understand. Believe in your relationship and in your love. And trust me, life will be beautiful once again," I finally concluded.

"I never knew you could be so deep in your thoughts. I am glad that I have a friend like you. Otherwise people give exactly the opposite advice," she said, keeping her hand on mine.

"Thank you, I am really happy that my words made some sense to you."

"Some sense? I am convinced that our relationship will be back on track, once again."

"I look forward to that day. And trust me, that will be one of the happiest days of my life too," I said.

"And I will look forward to the day when you and Anamika meet again. You will be together forever. That would be the happiest day of my life, Kabir," Yamini said, keeping her hand on mine.

"I am sure we would meet. The question is 'when'."

"Soon, Kabir. God can't keep people like you away from their soul mates for a long time. He is just checking how strong you both can be during difficult circumstances so that you both can support each other for the rest of your life."

I smiled because I knew the time was about to come when we would be together, forever.

# 29

## *Anamika*

**Hospital, Midnight**

It's been almost a day since I have been on this bed, unconscious during most of the hours. In between, whenever I was a bit conscious, I tried to move my body. But, with the needles injected in my body, I was unable to move even by an inch.

People walked in and out of that hospital room where I had been admitted yesterday. With an oxygen mask on my face and the nurse coming to give medicines to me almost every hour, I knew I was in a critical condition.

It must be around midnight when I heard a few voices around me. I slowly opened my eyes and saw Dr Neha talking with another doctor, who looked much older and senior to her. She was addressing him as 'sir'. There were some papers in their hands that they were going through them.

"Are you sure, sir? I mean, is that the only option left?" Dr Neha asked the senior doctor in a concerned tone.

"Yes, Dr Neha. I have seen all her recent reports. You see this infection here? It's spreading and it's dangerous for her in this condition," he said, showing her the report.

"I know, sir. But, operating in this condition? She still has time... you know what I mean," Dr Neha said.

"I understand your concern, Dr Neha. But, that's the only chance and we have to take it," he said, looking at me with concern.

When he noticed that I was awake, he smiled at me.

"Don't worry! She is a fighter. We will try our level best. Rest is up to god," he said, looking at Christ's picture on one of the walls.

"So when do we operate on her?" Dr Neha enquired.

"In the next couple of hours. Say early morning? We cannot delay it any further," the senior doctor replied and turned towards the nurse. "Prepare for the surgery," he instructed and handed over the reports to Dr Neha.

Then, he walked towards my bed. "Get ready for the morning, fighter!" he said, looking at me and then he walked out of the room.

Dr Neha came and sat next to me. She looked worried.

"What happened, Dr Neha? You look tense," I asked slowly as I was finding it difficult to speak properly.

"Nothing! Everything is fine. We have gone through your reports and..." she fumbled.

"And what?"

"They are going to operate on you in the next few hours," she replied.

"So soon? I mean..." I wanted to speak, but she did not let me.

"Don't worry, things will be fine. They have gone through your reports and..."

"Is this the only way? Can't they just wait?" I didn't let her complete.

She didn't reply. Rather, she kept looking at me for a while. I understood her silence. I wanted to remove my oxygen mask and Dr Neha helped me with that. She placed another pillow behind my back for additional support and propped me up a little bit.

"All these days, I was waiting for this day, when all my pain and suffering would end forever. And today, when I know that it is going to end and a new journey is going to start, then why am I scared, Dr Neha?" I asked looking at her.

"You don't need to be scared. It's all in your mind."

"I understand what you are going through, but remember, I am here. I am here with you, my friend," Dr Neha said, keeping her hand on mine.

"Thanks, Dr Neha, thanks for the support that you have always extended," I said.

"You don't need to thank me. I have always told you that I am also your friend. You don't need to thank me," Dr Neha said.

"I am not being formal at all. I am just thanking a friend."

"If you really consider me as your friend, then can I please request something?" Dr Neha asked after a pause.

"Anything except that one request," I said.

"You know very well that I am going to ask you only that."

I didn't respond as I knew what Dr Neha was going to ask me.

"Why? Why are you doing this to yourself?" Dr Neha said, looking at my cold reaction.

"You know it very well, Dr Neha. It's not about me, it's about Kabir," I replied.

"I am tired of listening to this bloody answer, but not anymore," Dr Neha said and took out her cell phone.

"If you are not going to contact him, then I am going to do that. Let me make that one call right here in front of you," Dr Neha said and dialled someone's number.

"No, please. Don't do that. You will be ruining his life. Please stop! I beg you," I pleaded, my breathing became heavy and I was unable to breathe properly. Dr Neha immediately adjusted my oxygen mask and kept her phone aside.

"Are you okay?" Dr Neha asked.

I nodded yes.

"Stop doing this to yourself. You know your condition. You need Kabir by your side now. Please listen to me for once," Dr Neha requested.

A nurse walked in and informed us, "Doctor, we are ready. It's time."

Dr Neha and I looked at each other and couldn't say anything. I guess the nurse was right. It was time now.

We kept looking at each other and then, I smiled at her for the last time before entering the operation theatre.

# 30

## Eleven months later

"Are you sure you will reach on time, Kabir?" Shruti asked over the phone. I was about to leave for office to attend a meeting with an overseas client.

I was not late, but Shruti was a bit concerned because it was one of the most important meetings. Probably, my biggest chance to prove myself again and get back to my career.

Finally, Mr Taneja had agreed to assign me a big overseas client's assignment. The client's presentation was scheduled this morning at our office and looking at my preparation and research, I was confident that I would get this deal closed in our favour.

"Don't worry, Shruti. I will reach on time," I said, getting into my car.

"Great, then. I will see you directly at the office. I am just about to reach," she said.

"Sure, see you in half an hour. We will have an hour to do a quick last-minute discussion, if required."

"It is going to be a great day, Kabir," I told myself and started driving.

While driving, I tuned into FM to listen to some nice music and to get the city updates. In Mumbai, while travelling, FM channels are the best mode of entertainment.

"Welcome back on the show! This is RJ Aditi and you are listening to your favourite FM channel - the City Pulse.

"It's a wonderful Tuesday morning, and as you all know, every Tuesday, we have as guest, a real hero of our society. Someone who has contributed towards the well-being of the people," RJ Aditi said excitedly.

"Today, we are going to speak with one such person, who has not just raised her voice against girl child molestation, but has also done some fantastic work in the past few months to address this serious issue," RJ Aditi announced.

"Girl child molestation!" RJ Aditi's words drew my attention to Anamika instantly.

"Welcome to our show, Ms Akanksha," the RJ said.

"Some Akanksha," I thought.

"Thanks, Aditi," Akanksha said.

But her voice sounded very familiar to me.

"Is she? No no, she can't be." I convinced my mind and concentrated on driving while listening to this conversation at a higher volume.

"Ms Akanksha, please tell us something about your initiative - Prayas."

"Well, Prayas is an initiative to stop girl child molestation in India. Through our initiative, we also encourage rehabilitation of the girls who have faced molestation at an early age or are undergoing such a situation currently," she said.

She spoke once again and I recognized her voice. *How could I not?* That was Anamika! The girl I had been waiting for all these months! My heart started to race against the speed of the car.

"But did she say Akanksha?" I questioned my mind and stopped the car at the side as I was about the reach the Bandra–Worli sea link.

"Wow. So tell us... how did you come across this idea of creating awareness of girl child molestation through Prayas?" RJ Aditi asked.

"Honestly, there are so many young girls who are molested during their childhood or teen years, at times by their close relatives, by their neighbours and many more. But, because of the society in which we live and the traditions we have around us, they are scared to share it with anyone. Not even with their parents. Because of which, these so-called 'friendly molesters' feel that no one can stop them from doing so," she continued.

"There is nobody these girls can trust, no one who can give them the correct advice and save them from the situation. That is where Prayas comes forward to support these girls," she concluded.

"God, what should I do now? There she is! My Anamika." I murmured, getting restless just by listening to her voice again.

"Wow, that indeed is a wonderful initiative, Akanksha," RJ Aditi said. "But can I ask you a direct question?"

"I know what you are going to ask and I will answer it for the benefit of someone who might need our support at this point of time," the guest said sweetly. "They may get the courage to come forward after listening to this," she replied.

"Have you... have you also been a survivor in the past?" Aditi finally asked.

She didn't reply. There was silence for a couple of seconds before Aditi spoke again. "It's alright if you don't want to answer my question, Akanksha."

"Yes, I have been a survivor," she replied.

"Oh!" Aditi said. "Please tell me what happens after such things?"

"Depression, disturbed life, you don't trust anyone, lose your focus and you feel very negative about life," she said in a heavy voice.

I kept listening with bated breath.

"It is sad. But then, what is someone else's doing cannot and should not be the end of the world for you. How can one overcome all this?" Aditi asked

"You need support, a lot of support from your parents, from your friends, and most importantly, someone who can trust you and can accept you for what you are," she replied.

"And I know, that someone is me, Anamika," I said.

I sat there dumbfounded for a few seconds, but quickly got into action. I googled the radio channel's number, but when I dialled, the line was constantly busy.

"Damn it!"

I pulled my tie down and decided to drive to office. Not mine, but the office of City Pulse from where this show was being aired.

"I am coming, Anamika," I said, driving as fast as I could. I didn't want to lose her this time.

The show was still on and I was hoping it was not pre-recorded.

"We have parents listening to you right now," the RJ was saying. "There are young teenage girls and the entire nation listening to you. So tell us what message do you want to pass on to everyone?"

"Number one... speak up! Do not hide anything. Do not keep this burden in your heart. Do not feel guilty because by doing all this, you will be punishing yourself and not these monsters who should get punished instead," she replied.

"Come forth and tell your parents or friends so that these monsters get the message loud and clear," she replied.

"And number two?" Aditi asked.

"Don't run away from your life. It is your life and no one can control it. You have to take charge of your life and start living it. Whatever has happened is in the past. Listen to your heart! Don't build a wall around it. Let the inner voice of your heart reach your mind. Just live your life the way you want," she replied.

"So what if something like this has happened? It wasn't your fault, life will not stop. Please come out of that mental frame of feeling guilty and start living a normal life," she concluded.

'Oh my god, you still remember the words I told you the last time we were together,' I thought while I was driving to reach to the radio station office.

"Don't be quiet and don't run away from your own life. The message is loud and clear," Aditi summarized.

"Thanks for tuning into our show. The session was very helpful and I am sure we are going to raise our voice and talk out loud on this issue to create more awareness," Aditi said.

"Thank you so much for joining us on our show, Akanksha."

"Thanks for inviting me, Aditi."

"This is RJ Aditi signing off from the show. See you tomorrow, Mumbai. Stay tuned!" Aditi said, ending the show. Soon after, an advertisement started playing.

"Shit! The show is over," I said, just when I was about to reach there.

"I hope I don't lose her this time." I was worried

When I reached the office, my cell phone rang. I picked it up without looking at the screen.

"Kabir, where the hell have you reached?" Shruti shouted from the other end.

"Just reached," I replied, getting off the car.

"Reached where, Kabir?" she asked.

"To meet Anamika," I kept my answers short and ran towards the lift.

"Anamika? Where is she?"

"Here, at the FM office," I said, looking at the long queue waiting for the elevators.

"What? But we have a meeting right now. The clients are here—.

"Screw that meeting and ask the clients to fuck off," I replied, taking the stairs.

"Kabir, wait! Listen to me."

"Bye, Shruti," I hung up as nothing was more important to me right now.

"Anamika," I said, coughing at the reception.

"Who?" the receptionist asked.

"Oh, sorry. I want to meet Akanksha." I forgot that she had introduced herself by that name on the show.

"Who Akanksha?" she asked again.

"The girl who was on the show with RJ Aditi a few minutes back. Where is she, ma'am?"

"Oh! Sorry sir, we are not allowed to share any such information," she replied.

"What! But I know her," I said, looking at the girl helplessly.

"Then, you can call her on her mobile," she said in a very casual tone.

"Do you even understand what I am going through, ma'am?" I was furious at her casual answer.

"Sir, please... I told you we cannot share any information or let you in like this, unless you have an appointment or you've been invited," she said.

"I will see who is going to stop me today," I said, walking towards the entrance.

"Sir, please stop. Stop!" she almost shouted but I did not listen.

"Security, please stop him!" the receptionist shouted and came out from behind the reception desk.

Two guards came running but were unaware of the fact that I was a pahadi. They found it difficult to stop me.

It was all chaos, as people saw me rushing into the office and pushing away both the guards.

"Anamika... Anamika!" I started calling her name at the top of my voice as soon as I entered the office.

Hearing the dramatic scene unfold, many people got up from their places and gathered around me, but I was least bothered. I only wanted to see Anamika.

"Excuse me, Mister," a female voice got my attention.

I looked back.

"What's your problem?" she asked. I got hold of my breath, took a pause and asked.

"Who are you?"

"I am Aditi," she replied.

"You mean, RJ Aditi?"

"Yes."

"Thank god you are here, Aditi. That girl who was there on the show with you just now, I want to meet her."

"Who? Akanksha?" she asked.

"Her name is Anamika," I clarified.

"I think there has been a misunderstanding. There is no one called Anamika here."

"I know she is here. I don't know why she is calling herself Akanksha. I know this girl, Aditi." I tried with conviction this time.

"Listen, whatever your name is—"

"Kabir," I introduced myself.

"Yeah, listen Kabir. Whatever her name might be, as a policy of the channel, we do not allow anyone to meet any guest like this, unless they are invited," she said.

"But I know her, Aditi. It's about us…" I said.

"I understand. If you know her, why don't you call her? And anyway, she is not here in the studio with us," she said

"What? Has she left already? It's just been minutes that the show ended," I said.

"She was connected over a call. She was not in the studio," she clarified.

"What?" I felt disappointed.

"Yes! Now will you please leave so that all of us can get back to work?" she said, pointing at the crowd gathered because of the scene I had created. It looked so filmy.

Everyone was looking at me and here I was, thinking about what to do next because my heart kept giving signals that the girl on the show was definitely Anamika and not someone else.

"Aditi, please help me reach her. I have lost her twice before in the last three years. I don't want to lose her again," I said, joining my hands in front of her.

"We can't, Kabir. We have rules. Everyone, get back to work please," she announced and turned to leave.

"Rules? Do you think life runs on some stupid rules?" I shouted. Aditi stopped and turned towards me. "What about emotions, feelings and love? Do we have to surpass all these just because we have rules?" My tone was still loud.

"Rules are good to be followed, but not at the cost of someone's life," I continued. Aditi and others around me kept staring.

Within these four walls, you may be having a lot of rules, but do you even know that there is life outside these walls? That runs on love and emotions, and not on your bloody rules," I said, banging at one of the walls.

Everyone was silent. Aditi looked at me and must have felt something upon seeing my condition. She finally said, "Come with me!"

"Aditi, you cannot do this," a man with a huge tummy came forward.

"Sir, I know what I am doing. Let's just listen to what he has to say," Aditi replied.

"But we won't be able to justify..."

"Sir, few minutes please," she requested.

The guy agreed and the three of us went into a room.

I drank a glass full of water which was kept on the table.

"Are you okay?" Aditi asked.

"Yes, I am okay."

"So, tell us. Who are you and why are you here? Plus, what about this Akanksha or Anamika story? How do you know her?" She fired a round of questions.

"I will tell you everything, but just one request," I said, looking at both of them.

"Now what?" the guy asked.

"Do not think that I am narrating you some story. It's about us and I am damn serious about it," I said.

Aditi assured me and asked me to carry on.

I narrated the entire story, right from the beginning. How I had met Anamika in Darjeeling, how we narrated our stories to each other, how I started thinking about her after coming back to Mumbai, the day I met her again in Mumbai at that cafe, the places we visited in Mumbai and the good time we spent together, that evening at my place followed by the wonderful night. In the end, I told them how she had left me again with the letter.

Both of them did not speak a word. They kept looking at me like I was possessed. I couldn't blame them. It was a lot to process suddenly.

"You guys don't trust me, right?" I asked.

"I don't," Aditi replied. The guy sitting next to her was silent.

"I knew you wouldn't, no one would."

I took out Anamika's letter from my pocket and handed it over to Aditi.

"What is this?" she asked, looking at the letter.

"This is the only thing I have which proves that whatever I told you about me and Anamika is real and not a figment of my imagination," I said.

She started reading it. The way, her eyes were rolling and her expressions were changing, I was sure that she was convinced now.

"I don't believe this," Aditi said. I could see the sadness in her eyes.

"What?" The other guy in the room asked.

"Sir, whatever Kabir just told us is true, word by word. I think their story is real."

The guy took the letter from her and read through it.

"Sir, we have to help Kabir," she said.

"I know, but there are some company policies..."

"Sir, for once, let us leave the rules aside and look at life. We always obey rules. Let's support love this time," Aditi said, giving the letter back to me.

The guy thought for a while and finally said what I was dying to hear. "Okay, let's do this!"

"Oh, thank you, sir."

I had no clue how Aditi was planning to help me reach Anamika.

"But how will we do this?" the guy asked.

"I have a plan, sir. Kabir, are you ready?" she asked, looking at me.

"I am dying to be with her," I replied.

"Then, get ready, Kabir. It's time now," Aditi said getting excited.

RJ Aditi took me to another cabin where another live show was currently on air.

She spoke with the RJ who was conducting the show, and in no time, Aditi took charge of the console when an advertisement was just coming to an end.

"Are you ready?" she asked and pointed towards the big black pair of headphones kept in front of me.

"Yes, I am," I replied, wearing the headphones and came towards the mic. The advertisement ended and RJ Aditi got into action.

"Helloooo listeners, welcome back! You are listening to City Pulse, and once again, this is RJ Aditi. Yes, RJ Aditi, you heard it right. Now, you all must be thinking why I am back again so soon? It is not my show time, right?

"But don't worry, you will get your answers soon.

"I had to come back on the show like this because I want to share a true story with all the listeners," she continued in full excitement. She looked at me and went on.

"Yes, a story! Of two strangers, completely unaware of each other's worlds and the different journeys they both were going to embark on and never meet again.

"But it wasn't written in their destiny to complete the journey alone, because that Allah, God, Jesus or whatever you may want to call it, wanted their different worlds to become one. Hence, their story started, but did not reach a completion... until today," she said.

"A few minutes back, you were listening to Ms Akanksha, who spoke about the pertinent issue of child molestation. She also spoke about how support from family, friends and loved ones is most important in this situation.

"We have with us right now, here in the studio, someone who has really helped her in coming out of that bad phase of life. Someone who has pumped new life into her and someone who has loved her truly. Yes, it's their story," she continued.

"They met by chance one night and shared their stories with each other. Then, they continued their journey of life without having any information, contact or any mode of communication.

"But as I said, they were destined to be together and hence, they met again, spent time with each other and this time, enjoyed each other's company and fell in love with each other.

"But hey, wait, wait, wait!" She said for effect. "Before they both could realize that they were in love with each other, thinking about her past, the girl decided to move away from his life without telling it to the person who loved her the most. For years, he looked for her everywhere, but couldn't find her. But he knew that he would find her, because they were destined to be together. And today, after almost two years, through our show, the guy found that girl again. Yes, you heard it, listeners!

"We have that someone in the studio right now. The guy who looked for that girl for years, but couldn't find her anywhere and yet loved her truly, even though she wasn't with him. Isn't that true love?" Everyone was listening to RJ Aditi carefully.

"So, here he is! Introducing Kabir, the reason behind Akanksha's happiness.

"This break in the show is about Kabir and Akanksha, aka Anamika's story that I am talking about. It is going to take a new turn from here. But this time, the turn will be a good one," RJ Aditi announced, looking at me.

"We are going to connect Kabir with Akanksha right now, live on this show so that Kabir can express his feelings. I am sure she won't turn him down this time.

"So, hold on, listeners! For the first time ever, a proposal on a live air show. And why not! After all, it's about true love."

She took a deep breath and dialled Akanksha's number.

The phone was ringing and my hands were shaking.

"Hello?" a girl picked up on the other end after a long ring.

"Hi Akanksha!" RJ Aditi said.

"Who is this?" she asked.

"This is RJ Aditi from Mumbai. We were live a few minutes back."

"Oh yaa, hi Aditi! I thought the show was over," she said.

"No, it's not over yet," Aditi said, looking at me.

"Oh, do you have more questions?" she asked.

"Not me, but I have someone who has been waiting for a long time to get some answers from you."

"What are you saying? Who is waiting?" she asked, sounding surprised.

"Wait, let me connect you. But before I do that, let me inform you that it's a live show and all our listeners are listening to you. So be honest while you answer this person," Aditi said.

"What's going on, Aditi? Who is there with you?" The girl on the other end was getting irritated now.

"Go on!" Aditi signalled to me. I took a deep breath and finally spoke.

"Hello."

"Who is this?" she said, trying to recognize the voice.

"Should I address you as Akanksha, or should I call you Anamika?" I asked.

For a moment, there was no reply from her. She took a pause. Aditi bit her nails and looked at me, waiting for a response from the other end. The entire office and the listeners outside were waiting for this conversation to move ahead.

"Kabir? Is that you?" she finally spoke.

Aditi's eyes sparkled with joy.

"Thank god you at least remember me!" I spoke.

"What are you doing there with RJ Aditi? What's going on, Kabir?"

"Too many questions," I said.

"Kabir—"

"I will answer all your questions, Anamika, but first, you answer my questions." I stopped her in between. "It's been close to two years since you left me in that situation. And you really don't know what I am going through. So please, for god's sake, please answer me from your heart this time," I said.

There was no answer from her side.

"Answer me, what should I call you? Anamika or Akanksha?" I almost shouted.

She spoke in an honest tone now, "For you, I am Anamika, and for the rest of the world, I am Akanksha," she answered.

"Why did you hide your real name from me?" I asked.

"So that you could never find me," she answered.

"Why you didn't want me to find you?"

She did not reply.

"Answer me, Anamika," I said.

"Because I fell in love with you, damn it! And I didn't want to get hurt," she answered.

"And how did you decide that you will be hurt?" I asked.

"I had written in that letter Kabir that I wanted love, and not sympathy. Also, what if you leave me someday and—"

"What if because of your past I walk away from your life some day? Leaving you alone again, right?" I completed her sentence.

"Yes," she answered.

"Oh, Anamika! How could you think like that? Right from the time we met in Darjeeling, I always had a feeling that there was something between us. But I did not know at that time what it was. But after we met in Mumbai, and the wonderful time we spent together made me realize that I wanted to hold your hand for the rest of my life. You were the one I was destined to be with till the last day of my life," I continued. "Yes Anamika! Till the last day of my life, and I mean it.

"But no, you chose to disappear from my life, leaving me with a piece of paper, just because you thought I was being sympathetic to you. And you presumed that one day I would leave you. Bullshit!" My anger and frustration came out this time.

She was quiet.

"Since the time we met, you never told me about the place you belong to, your family or your friends. You left no clue for me to come and find you, but still, for the last so many months I have been going crazy, looking for you everywhere – Mumbai, Darjeeling, in monasteries, and god knows where all. I couldn't find you anywhere. I spent most of my days at either Gateway of India or at the Siddhivinayak temple, hoping that I would meet you there again, someday."

"Kabir," she wanted to speak, but I wasn't done yet.

"People around me started thinking that I had gone mad. I almost had a nervous breakdown. I had started looking sick and was almost fired from work. And you thought it was sympathy... a temporary feeling which would vanish some day?" I concluded.

"Oh Kabir, I am really sorry. I didn't know that I made such a big difference to your life. I found myself back because of you, but didn't know that because of me, you would lose yourself," she said in a heavy voice.

"Almost lost," I said.

"So, now what?" she asked.

"Anamika, you had once told me that if it was written in our destiny to meet again, then we would meet for sure. Here is our destiny, right in front of our eyes," I replied. "A life full of happiness and togetherness is waiting for us. The path is clear, Anamika. We just have to hold each other's hand and walk over it to enjoy the rest of our journey together, forever."

She broke down and started weeping.

"Don't cry, Anamika! Please tell me, are you ready to hold my hand for the rest of this journey?"

She did not respond. RJ Aditi unmuted her mike and took charge to speak with Anamika.

"Tell him, Akanksha! Sorry, Anamika. Tell him that you are ready. We all want to know your answer," RJ Aditi said excitedly.

"Tell him that you love him and are ready to hold his hand. Trust me, we have many girls waiting outside this door and probably many listening to us right now who are looking for a guy like Kabir. Someone who can love them so truly and unconditionally," she said and everyone started laughing.

"Tell me, Anamika. I am waiting for your answer," I asked softly.

"I love you, Kabir," she said finally.

The crowd gathered outside Aditi's cabin cheered out loud. Aditi signalled me to speak those magical words to her.

"I love you too, Anamika," I said.

In excitement, Aditi gave me a tight hug.

Finally, I had found her. The time had come for us to be together. Time to celebrate life. We had waited enough for this, but this was bound to happen. Because as Aditi said, someone called Allah, God, Jesus and even our destiny wanted us to spend the rest of our life together.

The crowd outside was still cheering for both of us, hooting and clapping. That's when I spoke again.

"Can I ask you one more question, Anamika?" I said.

"You know I don't like to be questioned," she said, reminding me of our initial conversation.

"And you know that I like to find all the answers," I replied.

"You know all the answers now, Kabir. I have answered all your questions, and that too, in front of an entire city," she said.

"But still, only one more question, and it's really important," I said, getting serious.

"What is it now, Kabir?" she said, getting a bit serious too.

RJ Aditi looked at me questioningly, the crowd outside became silent once again and waited for me to ask that one important question. Everyone's eyes were on me. There was silence once again.

"Anamika," I said.

"Yes, Kabir?"

"I wanted to ask you..." I stopped.

"Go ahead Kabir, I am listening."

"Where do you live, Anamika?"

Aditi and the crowd outside started laughing.

"Answer me, because I am dying to see you," I said.

"Chandigarh," she replied.

"I am coming there," I said and rushed outside the room.

The FM was still on as I was driving to the airport. I was finally going to meet my mysterious girl.

"Wow, that was truly an amazing story. Wasn't it, everyone?" RJ Aditi was still on air and now concluding the show.

"After listening to their story, I feel that something called true love does exist. Earlier, I used to listen and read about love in movies and books, but never experienced it. I always had doubts about this thing called destiny and never believed in it. But, I was so wrong. Today, in this studio, I have not only seen what true love is all about, but also seen destiny taking shape.

"What I have understood from Kabir and Anamika's experience is that we don't have to go anywhere to find true love. The invisible powers around us have already planned our journey. Sooner or later, we will find our soul mates.

"So listeners, keep believing in the magic of love and don't lose hope. Because at times, what we perceive to be an end can actually be a beginning of an exciting life.

"This is RJ Aditi signing off for the day. Enjoy your life, keep loving life and be hopeful, no matter what. If you are destined to be with someone you love, then your destiny will find a way to unite you with them."

# *Epilogue*

## Two years later

Anamika looked beautiful in a pink chiffon saree with her hair open and a few accessories that she wore. She was the prettiest girl I had ever seen. She was sitting next to me, looking at the stage, eagerly waiting for the big announcement. I looked at her, thinking about my life and the endless happy moments that she had added to my life.

Yes, it's been two years since I met Anamika again in Chandigarh and that was the most memorable day of my life. That day, when we finally met, all our pain and sufferings had ended. It brought back the joy of being with the love of my life forever.

I was thrilled upon seeing my little angel, my daughter Anaayrah, for the first time that day in Chandigarh.

Yes, my daughter Anaayrah. Our daughter!

In spite of having so much trouble, she went ahead against everyone's advice of terminating her pregnancy. Everybody, including Dr Neha, wanted her to rethink her decision, but Anamika was adamant. She was firm on her decision of bringing our child into this world because she believed that giving life to our child was the only way to start a new life. She knew that with a child in her life, she would always be able to breathe in her life. She would always have a motive to cherish the rest of her life.

The journey was not easy. She knew that without me, she was all alone. But, she has always been a fighter. Despite critical complications in her health and the severe infection in the eighth month of her pregnancy, Anamika endured all the pain and suffering and gave birth to our beautiful angel, Anaayrah.

What an amazing life partner I have in my life! I was looking at Anamika and then at our little Anaayrah, who was sleeping peacefully on my lap. Along with Anamika and Anaayrah were seated Maa, Pavan, Shruti, Yamini and Mr Taneja. We were all waiting for the big announcement.

Yamini had finally expressed her feelings to Mr Taneja, and for the first time in life, Mr Taneja kept emotions on top of his business. They both started living a happy life. They started exploring the world together and had come especially for this big event.

On the professional front, Shruti is now the new creative head of BIM and enjoys her professional career. She, too, has started believing in the power of destiny.

Maa is extremely happy with my decision of returning to Manali. After all, along with me and Anamika, she gets to enjoy her time with her sweet little granddaughter.

Anamika continues to work towards her initiative, Prayas, and has opened support centres in various cities in order to prevent girl child molestation.

Pavan, Anamika and I often go on unexplored treks, connect with nature. Sitting on a high hill, we breathe in life together.

I looked at them who, in some way or the other, had played an important role in shaping my destiny. I was truly blessed to have them all in my life.

I was lost in thinking about my life when the announcement, that Anamika had been waiting for, was finally made.

"And the Bestselling Author's award for this year goes to Mr Kabir Shergill, for his debut novel *The Girl I Met That Night*," the emcee announced and the crowd cheered.

"You did it, Kabir!" Anamika said as my name was announced.

"Love you!" I said, giving Anaayrah to her and kissed Anamika on her forehead before walking up the stage.

"Since I was fired from work, I dedicated myself and followed what I wanted to do since years - writing a story and turning it into a beautiful book," I spoke from the dais. "People around me thought I was making a mistake, and they were not wrong. I mean, I could have easily grabbed another job and could have lived happily, accepting that as my destiny.

"But there she was, my inspiration!" I said, looking at Anamika. "She knew what I wanted in life and she supported me unconditionally. She was with me on this journey, holding my hand and having complete faith in me.

"She knew what I was writing; she had to. After all, it was our story," I said, looking at Anamika.

"And here I am, standing in front of you all, receiving this award for the bestselling author of the year. With readers from every corner of India and abroad showering their love on this book, and with the love of people like you all sitting in this auditorium, I have finally made a mark for myself," I said, showing the award trophy to the audience.

"Thank you, readers, and thank you all for making *The Girl I Met That Night* the number one bestseller of the year. It wouldn't have been possible without the support of each one of you. Thank you all, from the bottom of my heart.

"Last but not the least, I would like to thank the mysterious girl of my life, Anamika. Yes, that's what I call her still. Thank you for coming into my life, because without you, this journey would not have been possible," I said, looking at her.

She blew me a flying kiss in return.

The audience applauded as I finished my vote of thanks and walked down from the stage.

"Good speech, Kabir," Anamika said, adjusting my tie.

"Thanks," I said, handing over the award to her.

"It's beautiful!" she said

"Indeed, beautiful," I said, looking at Anaayrah.

"I am talking about this award," she said.

"And I am talking about the two awards that I have got in my life," I concluded, looking into her eyes.

"So, what next?" she asked.

"Hmm... a long break. Somewhere on an island or at a peaceful place, just you, me and our little bundle of joy. Let's see what's written in our destiny next!" I replied, holding her hand.

"Sounds interesting. I am sure our destiny won't let us down," she said.

"Having you beside me, Anamika, I am sure there is only more love, more happiness and togetherness in our destiny."

"Let's go, then!" she said, holding my hand as we walked out of the auditorium to head for the most beautiful journey of our life.

Our family and friends were still cheering and clapping for us. Shruti and Pavan, standing next to each other, were looking at both of us with utmost happiness.

"Can't believe that in today's time, we still have such true love alive," Shruti said.

"Even I never believed in such true love, but looking at both of them, I am convinced that if there is true love written in our destiny, then one day, we will meet our soul mate," Pavan replied and Shruti nodded in agreement.

"Seems like you haven't met your soul mate yet," Shruti asked as they walked outside.

"Not yet. How about you?" Pavan asked Shruti. She only looked at him without any response. Pavan understood her silence.

"So, you believe in destiny, haan?" Pavan asked slowly and looked into Shruti's eyes.

Their eyes met. There was a spark. They both kept looking at each other and smiled.

***"At times you find destiny. At times, destiny finds you."***

*Till then,*
*Keep Breathing Life!*